INTERFACE

THE NARAVAN CHRONICLES 2

ISABO KELLY

T&D
PUBLISHING

INTERFACE

Published 2018 by T&D Publishing
Cover design: © 2017 EJR Digital Art
Interior book design © 2018 T&D Publishing
ISBN-13: 978-1-944600-11-2 (Trade Paperback Edition)

Originally Published in DREAM QUEST October 2003

This is a work of fiction. All of the characters, places, organizations, and
events portrayed are either products of the author's imagination or are used
fictitiously. Any resemblance to actual persons, living or dead, business
establishments, events, or locales is entirely coincidental.

First printing T&D Publishing edition: April 2018
For information, contact T&D Publishing www.tanddpublishing.com

To my family, because they stick by me. Thanks for the support and the laughs.

GINA PAUSED JUST OUTSIDE THE DOOR OF HER FATHER'S private office when she heard strange voices from inside and listened to make sure she wasn't interrupting an important meeting. The door was cracked an inch, not enough to see into the room but enough to hear the conversation.

A conversation she couldn't believe she was hearing. She dug ruts in her palms with her nails as she tried to contain her temper.

"Gina won't like this," her father said. "Getting her to agree to added security is never easy, but this…" His voice dropped. "She doesn't know about the threats. I didn't want to tell her everything."

"Is that wise?" a male voice asked.

"No. Not with her temper. But she'll just have to understand. I won't take any chances now. Not after that last message."

You won't take any chances? Gina sucked in a breath through her teeth. *This is my research.*

"Do you have any idea who the outside source is, Mr. Xanacovich?" another male voice asked.

"I can't imagine who would do something like this."

"With Xanac Corp's ties to the initial development of detectors," the first man said, "it could be a Shifter terrorist group."

Gina sucked in a silent breath. Shifters were an alien species of shape shifters native to Narava, and detectors were the only way to identify them when they weren't in their natural forms. She still had mixed feelings about the part her family's company had played in the development of detectors. Their research had led to a number of advances, including a way to scan for a Naravan-based blood virus that had killed many Naravan's over the years. But the DNA based scanning technique had also greatly advanced the development of detectors. While this meant Shifters couldn't just *be* anywhere they wanted without humans knowing, it also meant they couldn't hide from human fear.

According to government research, though in her opinion "research" was a very loose term for what they did at Shifter Research Center, Shifters were a dangerous, parasitic animal likely to wipe out the human population on Narava if not countered. Silly idea since humans had lived on Narava for fifty years before even knowing the Shifters existed. And even if they could potentially be dangerous to humans, the only species currently on the verge of being wiped out were the Shifters. The illogic of SRC's arguments kept Gina from believing most of what they said, and she felt for the Shifters, being driven so close to extinction because of bad science.

Still, a huge portion of the population agreed with SRC. Most people were terrified knowing a Shifter could be in their home or next to them on the street without them knowing. So Shifter exterminations had been legally sanctioned.

But not everyone agreed with the government's actions. A few small pockets of humans advocated an end to the exterminations and were brave enough to come out publicly in support of ending the slaughter, even knowing it was dangerous to take that stance. She hadn't mustered up the courage yet, but she admired those who had.

Rumors had been flying over the last two weeks about the findings of an undercover Guard concerning Shifters and one of the Shifter support groups. Each side of the volatile argument assumed the Guard's report would support their view— either to continue the exterminations or to end them. She was hoping for the latter.

"Xanac Corp's contribution to the development of detectors was minimal, and before my tenure as CEO. Why hit our R&D team now?" Her father's voice was quiet, strained.

"To highlight their cause?" the first unfamiliar voice said. "To move interest away from this the rumored Guard report to a topic more immediate?"

Despite her growing anger at being left out of this important conversation, a conversation involving her research team, Gina found the timber of the stranger's voice flowing like heady liquor through her blood stream. Whoever he was, she could listen to him talk for hours. He had the kind of deep, rhythmic voice that reminded her of dark nights, tangled, sweaty sheets, and murmured desires.

"That situation only started two weeks ago," her father said, referring to the undercover Guard. "I've been getting threats for a month."

"The threats are to get you to stop the work, so…something directly to do with the research then? And how it relates to the Shifters?"

Gina's eyes widened. Had her father told the two men *everything* about her work? She ground her teeth together.

"No. This wasn't done by anyone supporting the Shifters," her father said, closing the subject with that obstinate there-will-be-no-further-discussion tone that drove Gina nuts.

There was a pause, the silence heavy. She felt a vein throbbing in her temple. She tried relaxing her clenched fists. *Calm, Gina. Just stay calm.*

"Under the circumstances, it's best if the regular security staff don't know about you," her father said, his voice authoritative but rushed.

"We understand, Mr. Xanacovich," the first man said. "Discretion's our specialty."

Discretion? This was what her father called discretion? Hiring perfect strangers then telling them about her work? Keeping threats to her research a secret? She struggled to contain a string of Deven curses. She always turned to her mother's native language when Naravan or Trade curses weren't strong enough. She took a deep breath, let it out slowly, and tried one last time to reign in her legendary temper. This wasn't the first time her father had gone behind her back to protect her. It was, however, the first time he'd kept the reason for his actions a secret.

She rolled her shoulders and focused on keeping her breathing steady. She would just walk quietly into the room, ask in a reasonable manner what her father was doing keeping these threats a secret from her. She could be calm and controlled when the situation called for it.

Unfortunately, this wasn't one of those times.

She slammed the office door against the wall with enough force that it echoed as she stomped into the office.

"What the hell's going on, Dad?"

Hands planted on hips, she took in her father's two guests with a scowl. The one standing was tall and muscular, his long black hair pulled back in a low tail showing a face so handsomely chiseled it was almost unreal. His hazel eyes narrowed at the intrusion. She flashed him a narrow-eyed look in return and got a raised brow in response.

The other man sat in a chair in front of her father's desk. She met a pair of deep blue eyes, and it took her a moment to remember to scowl. *He* wasn't too handsome, not by a long shot. But he was very male. Tawny hair, strong features, wide shoulders, a heart-stopping mouth. A shiver of electricity skittered up her spine as her gaze locked on that mouth.

He's the one with the sexy voice, she thought before she could stop herself, and her stomach muscles tightened in anticipation of hearing him speak through those deliciously captivating lips.

With a disgusted grunt, she pushed the physical reaction aside, calling up her anger. Now was not the time to worry about the faint smile curving the man's tempting mouth, or her suspicion that he knew exactly what she'd been thinking.

"Well?" she directed her ire toward her father.

"Gina." He straightened in his seat, emphasizing his height the way he did when he was nervous. "What are you doing here? I thought you'd still be at the labs."

"Obviously. But I'm not the one who needs to answer questions. Why didn't you tell me you were receiving threatening messages?"

"I didn't want you to worry." Her father raised his hands, palms out, trying to placate. Gina wasn't in the mood.

"Worry me? I'm not worried! I'm pissed off. How dare anybody threaten you to get me to call off this research? You can just tell whoever it is to forget it. They think they can hurt me? I dare them to try."

She didn't miss that interesting mouth trying to suppress a grin. She just chose to ignore it.

"Honey, you don't understand. These aren't nice men we're dealing with here. You can't possibly—"

"And why not? I bet I've got as much hand-to-hand training as these two thugs you're hiring."

"It's not a matter of training. Self-defense classes are not the same—"

"Self-defense classes? I'm a black belt in karate. I can handle myself, and you well know it."

"All the training in the world can't stop an unexpected blaster shot from ripping through you." The deep, slightly amused comment came from the seated man. And she'd been right. His voice eased through her, tingling across her nerves, and settling into her bones. That voice could conquer worlds. But his comment spiked her already raging temper.

Gina turned her anger on him, but before she could launch into a satisfying tirade, her father spoke.

"I don't care how much training you've had or how well you think you can take care of yourself," he said. "That has nothing to do with this situation. Haven't you noticed, damn it? You're one of the brightest women I know, and you haven't figured out yet that the others were not accidents?"

Not accidents? "What do you…" She stopped. For a moment, all she could do was stare at her father, anger dissipating beneath the shock of facts. Jesus, how could she have missed it? The rash of accidents in the last month, the injuries, the deaths…

Two of the original group, the only other two besides her and Jack Nevel who'd actually participated in the experiment, were dead. But Mira and Barry had died in a public link accident that killed fifteen people. The other accidents… Serious injuries, property damage… All members of her research team directly connected to the experiment.

Gina's stomach flipped. It couldn't be. She had to be wrong. There was no way the accidents could be anything other than an unfortunate set of coincidences. "What makes you think they weren't accidents?" she demanded, not willing to believe without proof.

Her father sighed and signaled to the seated man. "Mr. Alexander."

Gina watched warily as the man rose and handed her a messaging pad. She stared at the fist-sized screen, looked up at her father then pressed the pad to activate the recall. Five messages scrolled past, each one more graphic and threatening, each one very specific in relating the details of the events of the last month. They left no room for argument. Someone was attacking her team. As she numbly read the final letter, she realized it detailed first the death of Jack, then her own death. She swallowed hard and handed the pad back to the still looming Mr. Alexander.

"Jack?" Her voice echoed, hollow in her own ears.

"His body was found yesterday evening."

Gina looked up into Mr. Alexander's blue eyes without really seeing him. "And the M-SIDs?" She directed the question toward her father while still staring at the mercenary.

"There's every reason to believe they disassembled when whoever's doing this tried to extract them," her father said.

"What reason?"

"The…the blood found with Jack's… The blood contained traces of the magnesium-iron-eltranium alloy released when the M-SIDs broke down." Her father fell silent, then whispered, "Gina, Jack was tortured before they attempted to extract the micro-scanners."

Gina's world tilted sideways.

CHAPTER TWO

WHEN GINA BLINKED BACK THE BLACKNESS THREATENING
her vision, she found she was sitting in the chair Mr.
Alexander had abandoned. One of the mercenary's arms
circled her shoulders, holding her steady. She smiled up at
him, though she wasn't sure it was much of a smile. "Thank
you." His tempting mouth tilted up, but his eyes were creased
and serious.

"Does this mean you'll accept their protection now?" her
father asked.

She stared at his hands where they were clenched
together on top of his desk. What else could she do? "What's
the plan?"

"The plan, Ms. Xanacovich," Mr. Alexander said, "is to
put out a story that you've taken ill and are being closely
monitored by two of your mother's associates. We're the
associates. Your mother can't get back from Neros Seven and
the quarantine she's instigated there for another two weeks.

So she's asked Nate and me to monitor your condition and treat you."

"Do you have any medical training?" She directed her question to the dark haired man, too aware of Mr. Alexander's hand on her shoulder to dare looking up at him again.

"Alex is a trained medic, and I can lie well if I have to. My name's Nathan, by the way, Nathan Longfeather. And this is Johan Alexander. He prefers Alex." Nathan grinned at his partner.

"So, what will this plan, my being sick, entail?" Her voice grew stronger as she spoke, her nerve slowly returning.

"We'll transport you to a safe house and guard you until the person behind the messages is caught," Alex said in such a matter of fact way, she turned to gape at him.

"But, couldn't that take a while?"

"It could. If Nate and I weren't planning on tracking him down personally. Protecting you is only part of the reason your father has hired us."

"How long? Will I be able to continue my work? Where's this safe house?"

"Undetermined but not more than a month. No. And it's better if we don't tell you."

"A month!" She spun in her chair to face her father. "I can't stop this work for a month! The M-SIDs will disassemble in three more weeks. We'll have to start from scratch. That'll put us more than six months behind schedule. The Foundation is going to want to know what we've been doing with all their grant money for the last two years."

"I'll take care of business. You take care of you. It's not just the research that's at stake here, Gina."

Her father's quiet tone deflated her outrage, making her

slouch down in her chair. She didn't like it. In fact, she hated it. There was no way she'd be able to keep from working for an entire month. At least a month was the worst-case scenario. There was every chance that Alex and his partner were as good as they claimed to be. Why else would her father hire them? So they probably would find the person behind the threats and "accidents" in less than a month.

God, she hoped so.

"Why can't I know where the safe house is?" she asked.

When no one answered, she sat up straighter and focused the full force of her suspicion on her father.

The silence stretched, all three men exchanging a look she had every intention of overriding. Bad enough her father hadn't mentioned all this mess to her sooner—her life was in danger…had been in danger for a month now. There was no way they were going to keep anything else from her.

"Answer me, dad."

Alex answered instead, in that damned seductive voice of his. "Mr. Xanacovich suspects an informant inside your research team, someone unscrupulous enough to either sell information, or someone crazy enough to carry out these threats and warnings themselves."

"Impossible!"

Her father winced and looked away.

She scowled. Her father wasn't being logical. Someone inside the group doing this? That didn't make any sense. He was too worried to think this through. She looked up at Alex, still hovering close to her seat, his hand resting on her shoulder. Alex was a mercenary, detached from the situation. He had to see the idea of someone inside the group doing this was ridiculous.

"We do a thorough security and psychological check of all the researchers, engineers, technicians and staff before we hire them," she said. "Everyone was checked. Even I had to go through one when I started working for Xanac Corp. It's not possible someone inside the group is capable of this."

"Ms. Xanacovich, whoever's responsible for all of this knows the schedules of the staff, specifics about the habits, social life, and schedules of all the members of your team, details about the research you're working on, details that only someone inside the organization could have had access to. This doesn't mean someone in your father's staff is crazed or this vicious." Alex squeezed her shoulder, a gesture she was sure was meant to reassure and comfort but was more disconcerting than his logic. "But the information is coming from somewhere."

Gina clenched her teeth together, locking her jaw in an effort not to curse. Damn it. She didn't want to believe any of this. But how could she deny it? Her own logic was insisting Alex must be right given the facts he presented.

She turned back to her father. He looked pale and worn, the lines in his face deeper than a month ago. With a shock, she realized what he must have been going through for the last month, knowing his only daughter's life was in danger. Had he suspected all along that someone inside the organization was responsible for this? Had he been wondering for a month if he'd wake up one morning to the news that she'd been killed?

Her shoulders slumped. She couldn't put him through that any longer. Not now that she knew. She was going to give in to the whole scheme. Going into hiding for a month, with no work to do, knowing there was a lunatic somewhere out there threatening all the progress they'd made in the last two years, threatening her father, threatening her…it pissed her off. But unless she met the culprit face to face, she was going to have to resign herself to hiding and letting someone else take care of everything. For her father's peace of mind, if nothing else.

"The files?" she asked her father. Her voice sounded flat.

"They've been encrypted and locked away. We won't give up the work, honey. It's too important."

It was.

Gina sighed, finding a measure of relief in his assurances. Knowing the research would continue made it easier to admit defeat, to accept going into hiding.

"All right. When do we leave? Should I pack anything?"

The hand on her shoulder clenched, a movement so quick and subtle she could have imagined it. Then the touch was gone. Her shoulder was warm where Alex's hand had rested.

"Pack light," he said. "Anything you need later can be acquired."

"I need to close out a few things in the lab first. Then I'll head out to my apartment."

"We'll meet you at the lab, then and take you back to your place. After we finish up here with your father."

She nodded and stood.

Her father rose and came around the desk. He pulled her into a tight, quick hug and awkwardly wished her good luck. He seemed reluctant to let her go and at the same time in a hurry to see her gone.

She walked out of his office without looking back, but she called over her shoulder, "I'll see you soon, dad." She damn well would too, very soon, if she had any say in the matter.

ALEX WATCHED GINA LEAVE, flexing his fists. He continued to feel the soft firmness of her shoulder against his palm, and he had a hard time keeping his attention from dropping to her ass. But with her father in the room, he figured that wasn't a great way to endear himself to his new client. He'd give her credit though. The woman had spirit, a fire which sorely tempted him. All that intensity and fight was a challenge he was going to have a hard time resisting.

But he and Nate had a rule about sleeping with clients. And while very technically, Gina's father was their client, not Gina, he was pretty sure Nate wouldn't see things that way.

He turned back to face Mr. Xanacovich, keeping his expression neutral and professional. If he was lucky, Nate wouldn't notice anything either. He just had to get through this job, keep Gina alive, and catch the person after her. Afterward…

Well afterward, she wouldn't be a client anymore. And he wouldn't have to worry about his rule.

Outside, crossing through the open-air courtyard to the biotech labs, Alex scanned their surroundings. Neatly manicured trees and plants filling strategically placed wooden plant boxes, decorating the smooth white pathways without cluttering the open space. This time of the afternoon, only a few people walked through the area, moving swiftly between the various buildings that made up Xanac Corp's main complex. The area provided enough privacy that Alex felt free to speak.

"Sapphire Range?"

"Best option," Nathan agreed.

The safe house located deep in the Sapphire mountain range was about as far away from Capital as they could take Gina without actually leaving Narava. And the isolation would make finding her that much more difficult.

After a pause, Nathan said, "You gonna be okay on this one?"

Alex scowled but didn't actually look at his partner. Shit. They'd been working together for too long. The man could read him too well. That usually played in their favor, making the partnership flow smoothly and efficiently. At the moment, though, he hated that Nate saw through him. But he wasn't about to admit it.

"What the hell are you talking about?"

"You know what I'm talking about. And you know the rule about clients, Alex. It's your rule."

Alex let out a slow breath before answering, so he didn't say something he'd regret later. "She's not our client. Her father is."

"Alex…"

The warning in Nate's voice confirmed what Alex already knew. His business partner wasn't going to buy into that technicality. "Don't worry about me," he said, though with an edge of reluctance. "I can keep it in my pants for the length of the job. Have I ever broken the rule before?"

"There's a first time for everything."

"We do the job. Everything else is insignificant until it's done."

"I sure as hell hope you mean that."

Alex thought back to his first look at Gina Xanacovich, spitting mad, and so gloriously stunning in her wrath she took his breath away. The heat in those chocolate eyes was going to follow him into his dreams. Only she wouldn't be mad, and they'd both have a lot less clothing on.

He had every intention of seeing that fantasy become a reality. He'd made up his mind to seduce the sexy engineer a heartbeat after first laying eyes on her. Once the job was finished. During…

"I'll be fine," he insisted.

But as they neared her lab and his heartbeat picked up at the thought of seeing her again, Alex had to fight with his own conscious. He'd never lied to Nate before. He hoped he wasn't lying now.

CHAPTER THREE

Gina stared out at the mountain range rising up around the ship as it dropped slowly to a smooth, gray landing pad. Blue-white snow sparkled blindingly in the bright sunshine, making her squint. "The Sapphire Range? Why would you build a safe house here?" She looked toward where Alex piloted the small on-and-off planet vessel.

"Have you seen anyone else around?" he asked without taking his attention from the instrument panels in front of him.

She shrugged, conceding the point. Only the hardiest of human colonists had ever tried to inhabit this area of the planet. Most stayed near the temperate coastlines and the lush green ranges of the interior of the three main continents. If she were going to set up a safe house, she had to admit, she would have considered this desolate area of Narava's southern hemisphere, too.

Unfortunately, she hadn't packed for the snow. "I'm going to freeze my ass off out there."

A low noise that sounded suspiciously like a chuckled floated back to her from the pilot's seat just as the ship lightly touched down.

"Don't worry," Nathan said as he passed her on his way toward the rear cabins. "We've come prepared."

She scowled forward at Alex's back until he turned in his seat. "How prepared?" she asked.

"I intend to make sure you stay very warm."

She narrowed her eyes. Was that innuendo? She couldn't tell. His expression gave nothing away. But his voice… Ah, that voice. He could recite the periodic table, and she'd read innuendo into it.

Before she could embarrass herself, Nathan came forward with an armful of parkas, passing her one and Alex another before slipping into his own.

She snuggled the soft, thick material around her neck, and took a deep breath. "Okay. Show me my new home for the next few weeks."

The minute the ship's loading ramp started to drop, the frigid air rolled in to slap Gina in the face. "Damn," she murmured, and pulled her coat up over her nose and mouth.

From directly behind her shoulder, closer than she'd realized he was, Alex said, "You should feel it when it's really cold here."

"No thanks."

This time she was sure that soft, deep sound was a laugh. A laugh she could feel brushing along every inch of her skin.

To her surprise, he leaned in and reached into the pocket of her coat. "You'll want to wear these," he said against her ear.

A little breathless, she glanced down at the gloves he held out for her.

"It's not far to the airlock, but the gloves will be more comfortable."

"Thanks," she muttered, hurrying to pull on the thick material. His scent, a light, musky cologne she could place, curled around her even when he straightened away. She wanted to roll her eyes and fall back against his big body, to wrap herself up in that sexy voice of his.

But in front of her, Nathan pulled out a blaster just as the ramp hit tarmac, and she decided now was the exact wrong time to consider anything besides survival. She'd spent a lot of the last day trying to forget the details in the grisly note outlining her death. Nathan's weapon was a sharp reminder that she wasn't here on holiday.

She risked a glance back at Alex, not surprised to discover he had a blaster in hand too.

"I thought no one knew about this place," she said, nodded at his gun.

"No one does. This is just a precaution."

"You're not wearing gloves."

He glanced past her and nodded at the short walk to the building. "It's not as cold out there as it can get. I'll survive to the airlock."

Since she didn't want him to read anything into her concern, she faced forward again and followed Nathan out of the ship.

They hurried down the ramp and fast-walked to the smooth, gray metal door of the airlock. From the landing pad, it was impossible to tell what the complex looked like, but from the air, she'd seen a jumble of metal boxes stacked on a rare flat expanse of snow. The "house" was constructed of a gray material that blended well with the surrounding land-scape. She wouldn't have even noticed it if Alex hadn't pointed it out during their descent.

Inside, corridors lit by motion sensor lights led them deeper into the house. She kept track of her bearings, not wanting to be stuck in a place she couldn't find her way out from if she needed to.

"While you're here, it's better if you remain inside," Alex said, as if he'd read her mind.

"Why?"

"Beyond the weather? The house is fitted with a shield to help deflect any sensor sweeps. A human walking around outside without the protection of the shield could be located by a satellite or a high flying craft scanning the area."

"If no one knows about this place, why would anyone bother to look here for the safe house?" She heard the sarcasm in her own voice but couldn't stop it. Thinking about the danger she was in kept triggering her temper right along with her fear.

"It's a precaution," Alex said, his own tone neutral.

She wrinkled her nose. She was trying to pick a fight for no other reason than that she was scared and angry and didn't want any of this to be happening. "Fine," she said when she thought she could keep the sharpness from her tone. "I'll stay inside. Too damned cold out there anyway."

The two men led her into an area that looked comfortable enough, if not exactly homey. There were soft rugs in neutral colors covering hard gray floors, no decorations to disguise the gray walls, but there was a fully fitted out library, a kitchen, sitting room complete with multiple screens, and a nice sized bathroom.

Nathan peeled off to some errand of his own while Alex showed her to a small, functional bedroom.

"It's not fancy," he said, watching from the doorway as she explored the space. "But the bed is comfortable."

"It's fine," she answered without looking at him. The idea of Alex and a bed in the same room set off danger signals, so she kept her attention on the gray walls, the serviceable metal furniture, and the dark maroon curtains covering the small windows. Despite being inside, she still felt a chill in the air, which made her especially grateful the bed was decked out with a thick, cream and blue duvet.

ALEX WATCHED her pace around the small bedroom, and it was all he could do not to step inside, close the door, and take her into his arms. The bed was more than big enough to accommodate them and all the plans he had for her, plans he'd been much too preoccupied with during the flight here. He had her scent now, after allowing himself the pleasure of leaning in close on the ship to hand her her gloves. It was a subtle but odd mix of spice and floral that seemed to perfectly define the woman. He wanted more of that elusive scent, filling him up as he explored her contradictions. He'd had a hard time resisting one quick little taste of the skin beneath her earlobe, too. But between the cold and Nathan's presence, he'd managed to control himself. Barely.

She tempted him more than he'd guessed possible. He'd never had this kind of problem before. And he wondered what it was about her, exactly, that had wrapped him up so tightly.

Her bravery maybe? Watching her face the threat to her life without breaking was impressive. He wouldn't blame her for falling apart. He'd read the threatening letter. It was gruesome and detailed, the stuff of nightmares. Yet she hadn't fallen apart.

Oh, he could see her fear, though she tried to hide it. She wasn't immune to the seriousness of her situation. He felt it was the way she stood strong, trying to mask her worry, that had him wanting to comfort her. Her energy and strength were as captivating as anything else about her. Maybe more. She was stunning, yes. But he'd worked for beautiful women before. And not once had he had such a difficult time keeping his hands to himself.

Gina sparked more than just lust in him. She set off every protective instinct he had on a level he'd never experienced before. It pissed him off that someone, anyone, could make this strong, intelligent woman scared. And that triggered something deeper, something a lot more dangerous than mere desire.

He'd spent most of his career protecting people and things, guarding against attacks and threats. Yet for some reason, with this one woman, he wanted to protect her not because he was getting paid to, but because he *needed* to.

Nathan was going to kick his ass if he realized just how far gone Alex actually was already.

He watched her pull her parka tighter around her neck and said, "There are warm clothes in the closet." When she turned, he pointed toward the barely discernable door.

"Thanks. I'm going to need them."

Her comment reminded him of what she'd said on the ship about freezing her ass off, and he couldn't help considering that very ass, despite it being completely covered by the coat at the moment. She had a lovely backside, perfectly shaped. Exactly the right size to fill his palms. He swallowed to wet a suddenly dry throat. "Help yourself to whatever you want." Including me, he thought before he could censor himself.

His gaze moved over her body, and his imagination jumped to detailed thoughts of stripping her naked and making sure she was too hot to notice the chilled air. Being in a room with a bed just a few steps away wasn't helping his control. Neither was the fact that her scent was starting to fill the small room. Even from the safety of the doorway, the spicy floral mixture reached out to tease him.

There was no denying he wanted her, more than he'd wanted any other woman in a long while. But there was more than just lust mixing in his gut when he looked at Gina. It was going to get them all killed if he wasn't careful. Keeping her safe meant keeping is mind on the job, his hands to himself. And his dick in his pants.

Doing all that required he get out of this bedroom. Now. "I'll leave you to settle in and get comfortable." He left before she could say any more.

CHAPTER FOUR

Alex and Nathan stayed at the safe house for a day and a half, making sure the building was secure and no one had followed them. During that day and a half, Alex was nothing but professional with Gina, and his professionalism drove her nuts.

She should have been relieved. The last thing she needed at the moment was to jump into an affair with a virtual stranger. But something about Alex fascinated her, despite the dangerous situation she found herself in. She caught herself watching the way he and Nathan organized the security of the house, started the search for the person behind the threats and deaths, and generally worked together like they could predict the other's thoughts. She smiled when it occurred to her they reminded her a little of an old married couple, the way they functioned so seamlessly, often without having to say a word.

Beyond watching him work, Gina kept searching out Alex, looking for excuses to see him or talk with him about some random concern. She felt like a schoolgirl with a crush, which was so embarrassing, she kept trying to pick fights with him. Not once did he rise to the bait. Damn him.

Sometimes, she thought maybe there was more to what he said when they spoke, to the way he looked at her when she wasn't supposed to notice. He did hunt her down almost as often as she went looking for him. And once, she'd noticed Nathan scowling at Alex while he spoke with her, like Alex was acting odd. Yet nothing ever came of those moments. Alex continued to deal with her like a client and nothing more. Her combination of annoyance, relief and embarrassment from all this played havoc with her notoriously bad temper and did not leave her in a very good mood.

His lecture on the house rules and security procedures didn't help any. He was so damned calm, never losing his own temper, even as she lost hers when his lecture took on a condescending tone. Yes, she knew not to use the external communications system, no she wouldn't try to contact anyone, yes she would keep the place sealed, of course she'd keep the internal alarms online. How old did she look, five? He remained unaffected and reasonable the entire time—an attitude which infuriated her.

They had exactly two non-professional conversations. One, a brief twenty minutes during which she dragged out of him that he had a degree in archeology and hated beets. The other when he found her in the sitting room staring at a newscast.

The riot in Capital, in the business district, captured her focus so fully, she didn't even hear Alex come into the room. A group advocating Shifter exterminations met a group against them across a line of Guards. The shouting and yelling escalated to throwing debris over the Guards' heads, to throwing mini-fire bombs, to an all-out riot. Three people killed, twenty injured, rioting spreading throughout the district.

She hugged herself and wondered if her work would help the situation or make it worse.

"Are you okay?" Alex said as he stepped into her peripheral vision.

She shrugged.

"What's happened?"

"Riot in Capital. More rumors the Shifters communicate via telepathy."

She faced Alex to ask what he thought, but the expression on his face surprised her. "You're upset. Why?" she asked. He rarely showed more than a calm, capable façade. At the moment, he looked…mad? "The riots or the telepathy?"

His eyebrows rose a little, as if surprised she'd picked up on his mood. She didn't want to admit she'd been watching him that closely. But every time they were in the same room, every time his deep voice reverberated across her nerves, she found she couldn't look away, despite her best efforts.

She refused to make a fool of herself just because his voice made her knees weak. But that hadn't stopped her from studying his every expression. Or imagining what that tempting mouth of his might feel like against her skin.

After a few more minutes of watching the newscast, he finally answered her question. "Telepathy." He shook his head. "I can't imagine anything more disturbing or invasive. Would you want a dangerous animal to be able to read your thoughts?" There was something like fear in his voice. He shrugged and his expression lightened as he turned from the screen to face her. "At least they can't understand what we're thinking. That'd be worse, having your thoughts read by someone who could actually understand."

She bit her lip to keep from saying anything else. Fear as much as professional caution keeping her silent.

As she studied him, she wondered if he'd ever worked a case involving the Shifters, if there was anything personal in his views. But she didn't ask. She was afraid she wouldn't like the answer.

He left a minute later with a slight nod, and Gina found herself alone again, wanting to trail after him. She focused on the screen instead.

ALEX PAUSED JUST outside the door and looked back in at Gina. He had things to do, to make sure she'd be safe after he left. But she was like a siren, her mere presence almost impossible for him to resist.

The look on her face, that concerned, lost expression tapped his protective instincts mercilessly, urging him to hold and comfort. That urge was causing him as much trouble as the urge to push her against the nearest wall and kiss her until she was breathless.

Since they arrived in the Sapphire Mountains, he'd been trying to avoid too many personal conversations with her. The last thing he needed was to get too know her any better right now, to solidify how much he *liked* and admired her. She captivated him. Such intelligence and such a temper all wrapped into a sexy, sleek body.

She kept trying to pick fights with him. He knew it was

because she was scared and attempting to distract herself. Her efforts amused him so much, he kept looking for ways to irritate her so he could watch that spark of fire rise. He never took up her challenge and lost his cool, but he found himself thoroughly enjoying her frustration. He was more than happy to be her distraction. Though, if he had his way, he'd choose a different method of distraction—activities involving naked skin and a large, soft mattress.

Unfortunately, he couldn't indulge those urges, at least not until after they finished this job. A month had never felt like such an excruciatingly long time in his entire life. And that included the month he'd spent in a Binnean prison during his more…misguided youth.

They had to uncover the person threatening her life soon. He wasn't sure how long his control would hold out against his rising needs. As it was, Alex was following Gina around the compound like a fucking dog in heat. And Nate was getting pissed. He couldn't blame the man. He'd be pretty ticked off too if Nathan suddenly started panting after one of their clients, risking everyone's safety because he couldn't control his dick. There was a reason for their rule. And Alex had been the one to insist on it when they first formed their business partnership all those years ago.

Yet, as he stared at Gina while she watched the continuing riot news, Alex had to forcibly stop himself when he took a step back into the sitting room, back toward her.

With a silent curse, he stalked to the control room.

Nate looked up when he entered, and his slight frown turned into a full blown scowl. "Alex, you need to stay the fuck away from her."

"There's a riot in Capital," Alex said in an attempt to avoid another one of these conversations. He'd had to suffer through Nathan's scowls and lectures enough already. Even if the man was right, Alex didn't have to take the reminders gracefully.

"Anything that will affect us?" Nate asked.

"It was over the Shifters—supporter against haters. Rumors the Shifters communicate via telepathy still causing chaos. It shouldn't impact this job."

Nathan nodded, looking thoughtful.

And because it took his mind off Gina and Nathan's off the trouble Alex was in, Alex said, "Would suck if the telepathy part turned out to be true." He sat at the nearest console and pulled up some of the complex schematics, triple checking the locks that guarded the escape tunnels running underneath the house.

"Not sure what that has to do with us."

"You like the idea of someone reading your thoughts?"

Nate shrugged. "No. But I've got other things to worry about. I'm not really concerned with the Shifter issue."

Alex raised a brow. He knew that was a load of shit. But Nathan had been spouting that same line since they'd met in college, and Alex never pushed him or the topic. If Nathan wanted to deny his ties to the Farseakers, especially after the most recent issue with Kira Farseaker, Alex couldn't blame him. He'd put a lot of his own past behind him when he started working as a mercenary, a life and a negligently disinterested family he was better off without. He wouldn't deny his partner the same option.

"Still," he said, "the thought of something being able to see into my head that way…" He hated the idea. On a very visceral level. The one place he had complete privacy was his thoughts. Someone or something being able to breech that privacy turned his stomach. "Sounds pretty fucking invasive."

"Especially with where your thoughts have been," Nate muttered.

"Shut the fuck up."

Nate raised a brow, and Alex ignored him to stare down at the three-dimensional image of the complex floating above the console in front of him. Neither of them spoke much for the next few hours.

CHAPTER FIVE

T HE NEXT AFTERNOON, THE TWO MEN LEFT. A S N ATHAN packed up their gear, Alex pulled Gina aside for another lecture. She tried hard not to roll her eyes, but his tone set her teeth on edge.

"You really need to stop talking to me like I'm a child," she said, interrupting his list of safety rules. "I'm probably one of the smartest people you'll ever meet."

She was only half-teasing, still trying to get some sort of reaction from him. She was restless and nervous at being left alone in the middle of nowhere with only a few droids for company. And despite herself, she kept looking for a fight to defuse the tension. Since he wasn't cooperating, her irritation hadn't had a single outlet.

"I know you're smart," he said. Suddenly that deep voice was serious, and somehow far more intimate than before. "I also know you're strong. But I don't want anything happening to you. So you'll follow our rules while we're gone."

"Of course I will." She licked her lips and started to say something snarky but stopped when his gaze dropped to her mouth. The look was brief, but full of an intensity she hadn't seen from him before. Her heartbeat kicked up. She might have imagined the heat in his eyes. But she didn't think so. And for a breathless instant, she thought she'd finally broken through his professional distance.

"Here, I want you to wear this while we're gone," he said, breaking the spell.

She was both disappointed and relieved as the moment of potential passed and he eased back behind his neutral mask. She was toying with disaster, trying to get this man to react to her. It wasn't like her to play these games. But something about Alex pushed every button she had, and she couldn't seem to help herself.

He handed her a small gadget that was roughly the size, shape, and style of a wristwatch, but the face was blank.

"What's this?" she asked, staring at the little devise.

"A panic alarm. There's a guard nearby, if something happens. Just hit that and he'll get here to help."

"Who is he? And why isn't he going to stay inside the house? There's plenty of room."

Alex's expression was impossible to read when he said, "He has a better vantage from outside the complex. Don't worry, he's a close associate. I trust him."

She stared at the panic alarm, believing Alex and trusting him, despite how little time they'd spent together. But the alarm was another reminder of the death threat hanging over her. She'd been working hard not to think about that threat. Now a trickle of fear eased through her. The weakness embarrassed her as much as the way she was acting around Alex, so she tried to keep her reaction to herself.

But Alex must have noticed something. He reached out and touched her shoulder lightly. "I won't let anything happen to you, Gina. You can count on that."

She took a breath and let it out slowly, as a shiver crawled up her spine. She met his gaze and forced a smile. "I'm going to be bored out of my mind without anyone around and with no work to do," she said in an attempt to sound normal.

A very slight smile curved his lips. "I'm sure you'll find something interesting to think about while I'm gone. You'll have to tell me all about it when I get back." He nodded a farewell and disappeared down the corridor.

Leaving Gina once again wondering if he was just being nice or had he actually meant something more by that parting shot.

ALEX HAD NEVER HAD such a hard time walking away from anyone before. He wanted to turn back, to give her something to think about while he was away, the kind of kiss that would keep them both anxious for their next meeting.

He didn't.

He couldn't.

So, he continued out the airlock into the thankfully freezing weather and headed to his ship, not so much as looking back to see if she watched them leave.

He didn't speak to Nathan either as they readied the ship and Alex got them into the air, back toward Capital and the source of the threats against Gina. He was afraid his partner would hear more than he wanted to reveal if he so much as opened his mouth. So they returned to the city in silence.

The next few days were agonizing. They did everything they could to track and flush out the culprit. And they kept coming up against some serious blocks. Which meant whoever it was, they were a person in power. That didn't bode well. People in power typically wanted to remain in power and wouldn't hesitate to do whatever it took to stay there.

On the third day of futile searching, Alex paced the length of his office while Nate sprawled on the long leather couch. He'd always liked this room with its deep colors, soft leather furniture, and lack of clutter. But right now, it felt like a cage keeping him from returning to Gina.

"You know what we have to do," Nathan stated.

Alex ignored the comment. He knew Nathan was right. But he didn't like it. "Have you been in touch with Bin'Ral?"

"All's quiet at the house. No sign anyone has tracked it."

"Good."

"That doesn't solve our current problem, Alex. We've been at this long enough to recognize the signs."

Alex grunted, a noncommittal noise to give himself time to think of an alternative plan. Anything else. But Nate was right. They'd come up against the kind of blocks and walls only serious money could buy. Whoever they were after was powerful, wealthy, and perfectly capable of hiding behind those resources indefinitely. They hadn't even had any luck flushing out the mole on Gina's team.

They weren't going to find the ultimate threat if they couldn't even flush out the smaller threat within Gina's team.

But they had bait to bring at least one of the bad guys into the open.

"Her father won't approve this plan, Nate," Alex said as he continued to stalk the length of his office, passing in front of the couch without looking at his partner.

"Her father doesn't need to know this part. We do this, though, and we can get our hands on someone with information. We don't, we'll be spinning our wheels for the next three weeks, and getting nowhere. You know it. We've seen these kinds of blocks before."

Taking a deep breath, Alex admitted the truth. "You're right. But part of our job is to protect her. We have to be on sight by mid-day tomorrow." That was the only part of the plan that didn't make Alex's instincts rebel. By doing this, he'd get back to Gina sooner.

He'd been thinking about her constantly since they left the safe house. She'd invaded his dreams and haunted his days. And more than once he'd considered taking over for BinRal, being the one to stay in the mountains and protect her while the Binnean and Nathan hunted down the threat. Doing what they needed to do would allow him what he most wanted without Nate accusing him of going soft. It really was the best solution. Their only solution. And it would end the threat to her life that much sooner.

Everything about the plan should have made Alex happy. But it put Gina in danger. And that part still grated against his every nerve.

"Well?" Nathan asked, waiting for Alex's decision.

"Set it up. I'll get our gear together for the return."

Nate stood and put a hand on Alex's shoulder. "You know

this is the best plan, right? This will stop the threat quicker and get her out of danger."

"Yeah. I still hate it."

CHAPTER SIX

ALEX STOOD AROUND A CORNER, WATCHING GINA STALK THE corridor between her bedroom and the library. His heart beat faster as he watched those long legs pace. Forcing his gaze up, he saw frustration pursing her perfect, full lips and wanted to kiss away her agitation. He'd only been away from her for four days. Yet she was the best thing he'd ever seen in his life.

She tugged at the hem of the oversized sweater she wore. His sweater. He hadn't even remembered leaving it here, and he had no idea where she had found it. But the fact that she was wearing a piece of his clothing made his more primitive self growl with approval. She looked good in his clothes.

She'd look better naked.

The weave of the sweater wasn't particularly loose, he couldn't actually see through it. But the soft cream color gave the illusion of skin visible beneath. And all he could think about was stripping that sweater up over her head and baring all that delectable skin. He wanted to taste her so bad…the thought of it kept him rooted to his spot in the corridor, doing nothing but watching her. Because if he went to her at that very moment, he wouldn't be able to control his reaction. There was still danger. They still had a job to do. She wasn't safe yet.

But he wanted her so damned much he couldn't think about anything else.

She tossed her hair and grunted in irritation, a gesture that made him smile. What was she thinking about? What had her so restless? Boredom probably played some part in her frustration. But he hoped there was more to it, like she'd been thinking about him as much as he'd been thinking about her. If she had been, he'd be more than happy to alleviate her boredom.

Once the job is done, his conscious reminded him. Until the job was done, hands off. If Nate's plan worked, this job would be finished soon. Then all bets were off. And then he intended to make good on his personal plans for her.

Another minute passed before he gave in to his need to get closer to her. The reminder of the job at hand gave him some measure of control over his desires. He could approach her now without stripping her naked. Probably.

He stalked out of his hiding spot just as she turned her back to him, resuming the circuit toward her bedroom. The move gave him a lovely view of her perfect ass. Suppressing a groan, he decided he would probably never have complete control where this woman was concerned.

GINA PACED the length of the corridor between her

bedroom and the library. She was as restless and bored as she'd warned Alex she'd be. She wanted to work, used to the concentration it took to unravel the biotechnological problems she and her team of engineers struggled with every day. Without that focus, her usually busy brain turned into a bastion of completely inappropriate thoughts about Alex, and she couldn't find anything to distract her attention long enough to hold those musings at bay.

She'd tried reading, watching movies, she'd even started checking on the weather reports four or five times a day. Nothing helped. Her boredom always circled her imagination back to the big mercenary with the sexy voice and wouldn't let her forget about him for long.

When her thoughts did turn elsewhere, unfortunately it was to remembered details of the death threat against her. So, of course, in her efforts not to dwell on that topic, her mind returned to more pleasant but equally dangerous fantasies of Alex.

She was starting to feel a little obsessed. Did he realize he'd done this to her? Or was this madness all her own making?

Just the boredom, she assured herself. If she was able to work, or do…anything else at all, she wouldn't be thinking about the man all the time. She'd suffered four days of inactivity. Of course the wait and idleness were getting to her.

She tugged restlessly at the hem of the oversized sweater she'd borrowed to stave off the cold air that seeped into the building despite the climate controls.

"There's been no sign of anyone anywhere nearby for days," she whined out loud just to hear some sound other than her footsteps as she stalked the empty corridor. "Not even this supposed guard watching over me from a distance. I don't see why I can't go for a walk."

"You have no way of knowing if a spy satellite or a high altitude craft is scouring the area." Alex's deep voice startled her so much she pulled a string loose on the sweater.

"Shit." She tucked the string back into the weave. "You scared the hell out of me. What are you doing here already? I thought you'd be gone longer."

"So did I. Didn't you hear the perimeter alarms going off?" He moved close and grasped the string she'd snapped, idly toying with it.

Her heart started to hammer and not from surprise. Although surprise didn't help. She'd spent so much time thinking about him for the last four days, yet she was nowhere near prepared to actually see him in the flesh again. "No. I didn't hear anything." Was that her voice?

She was having trouble concentrating. The heat of his hand seeped past the loose weave of the sweater, tingling low on her abdomen. She could practically feel his touch on her skin even through the top of her jeans. And the sensation brought to mind too many of her recent fantasies. Her stomach clenched.

Alex frowned, seeming unaware of the mayhem he was causing her, damn him. "I'll check the system now. You should've heard something before I deactivated the alarms from the ship when we flew in." But he didn't move away to check the system. He stayed where he was, standing too close, staring down at her, his big body still except for the movement of his strong fingers playing with the hem of her sweater.

His nearness, his sudden appearance, the object of so

many recent lust-filled daydreams, was overwhelming her. She should tell him to step back. She should say something. He'd left her here without any communication for days, knowing she'd be bored. And despite some of her more fanciful moments before he left, he hadn't actually come out and admitted any interest in her. Letting him this close, when she was so on edge, was too dangerous. She was likely to do something extremely embarrassing if she didn't put some space between them. Now.

She lifted one foot, put her toe down on the ground behind her, intending to move away from him. Instead, she stayed where she was with her heel in the air, feeling like a magori-fox staring into the eyes of a cor-snake.

Put your foot down, Gina. Take the step back. She needed distance. To concentrate. *Say something. Tell him to back off, now. Tell him to stop teasing you.*

"Where's Nathan?" That wasn't what she wanted to say. Her voice sounded faint and breathless. Did he notice?

The curve of his fascinating mouth said he did. "He's checking the external sensors and alarms."

She wasn't sure how he managed it, but he seemed to suddenly be closer without taking a step. Had she moved closer to him? God, she hoped not! How embarrassing. He smelled wonderful—that same warm, musky cologne she couldn't put a name to but was now permanently tied with thoughts of Alex. What was he doing with her sweater?

"Any progress?" she asked, knowing her voice sounded weak but not sure how to clear out the webs of desire clouding her mind. Every time he spoke, her gaze dropped to his mouth. And that wasn't helping at all.

His faint smile turned into a crooked grin. "I'd say so."

"I meant about finding the person responsible for the threats." She felt her cheeks heat, knowing full well he'd caught her staring at his mouth. Again.

She was acting like a schoolgirl. This was silly. She barely knew him. He was too close, and she needed to move back.

But it was so good to see him. She hadn't even realized she wanted to see him this much. Okay, so she'd been thinking about him constantly since he left. Alex didn't know that. She had no reason to get embarrassed and shy. He couldn't realize she'd developed all those detailed fantasies of him over the last few days.

Could he?

What the hell was he doing with her sweater?

"We've made some progress on the threats," he said. "I've left a colleague to follow up a lead. I wanted to get back here to make sure you were all right." The hand playing with her sweater stilled. "Are you all right?"

The heat already coiling low in her stomach exploded lower. *Breathe, Gina. Breathe.* "I'm fine. I'm bored. Can I go back to work soon?" Her gaze darted down to where his hand still gripped her sweater. For a disorienting moment, she thought he might start to lift the sweater up, revealing bare skin beneath. Her gaze jumped back to his. Would he?

He grinned. "Soon."

Gina swallowed hard. Silence stretched between them. She felt like her balance was going, because she seemed to be tilting closer to him, the heat of his body drawing her, the tingles in her own body begging for his touch. She flicked her tongue out to wet dry lips.

Alex's voice was husky when he murmured, "Maybe there's something we can do about your boredom."

Her heart kicked over, and her stomach dropped. If he didn't mean what she thought he meant by that comment, she was going to scream. God, she really was leaning into him. She needed to move back. She still had one foot behind her, toe resting on the ground. If she just dropped her heel, she'd gain some space. That's all it would take, a little space between the heat of his body and her tingling skin, and she'd be able to think clearly.

She was a logical, rational woman—most of the time. She didn't fall for men she barely knew. This was just chemistry. And days of inactivity. He was good looking. She was bored. She could move away from chemistry. Drop her heel. Move away from temptation.

He bent closer, washing her lips with the warmth of his breath, and she leaned into him instead of away. "I've been thinking about you, Gina."

"You have?" Surprise and excitement swept into her bloodstream.

"Probably too much for my own good. But I haven't been able to stop thinking about you."

Her heart rate tripled. So she hadn't imagined those looks, the innuendo. That deep, husky note in his voice was a sign of more. She wasn't sure whether to cheer or turn and run from something so potentially dangerous to her peace of mind. What she actually did was let her lips brush ever so slightly against his.

CHAPTER SEVEN

Alex breathed deeply. Her heat, her scent... They seeped into him, making him forget everything else going on around them. All he could focus on, all he could see were her lips, so close, so so tempting. When she leaned in, when her mouth moved against his, he lost all hope for coherent thought. His hands flexed, and he reached out to pull her close, to take that brief contact into the full kiss he'd been desperate for since first meeting her.

Before he could make good on his impulse, though, the sharp echo of footsteps caused him to jerk his head up. Gina looked past him, her eyes dazed, and he had to resist the urge to kiss her again. When she rubbed her lips together, he suppressed a very primal groan.

Fully intent on finishing what was just started as soon as they had some privacy, he gave her a wry grin then glanced over his shoulder, knowing Nathan was the one who'd interrupted them. When he saw the expression on his partner's face and the blaster in Nate's hand, he pulled his own weapon, instantly on alert.

"What's wrong?"

"Did you check the perimeter alarms yet?" Nathan's eyes flicked to Gina then focused on Alex.

Alex shift, just a little, as guilt poked a hole in his lust. "Not yet."

"An area of the external sensors has been blasted out. Not subtle. And they're fresh. Maybe only ten minutes, twenty before we landed."

"Damn." A hint of fear snuck in with his guilt. He'd been so distracted by getting his hands on Gina, he'd failed to follow his own damned safety procedures. And now she was in real danger. At least their original plan had worked. It just worked too fucking quickly. They weren't ready. Which changed everything. "Have you signaled BinRal?"

"He's on his way in. Now what?"

"I'll get her out of here while you search the interior. We'll meet in the ship. Lifting out in twenty."

"BinRal?"

"I'll intercept him on the way. He should have enough time to sweep the area and still make it to his ship before we blow the place."

For the first time since Nate's arrival, Gina spoke. "Blow the place! What do you mean 'blow the place'?"

He spared her a glance, his mind already on the things they needed to do to get her out safely, even as he tried to push down the guilt rising up to taunt him. "This house has been compromised. We have to abandon it. But we can't leave it intact. There're ways a smart person could use the computers here to track down some of our other retreats. We can't allow that."

"But…but there's someone here already. And you're only giving us twenty minutes to get away."

"Don't worry," Nathan said, moving back down the corridor. "We've handled situations like this before."

Alex took her arm with his free hand and led her toward her bedroom. He kept his blaster raised, scanning the area as they moved. He couldn't believe he'd endangered her because he couldn't think beyond his own needs. He cursed silently as they reached her room and she moved inside to collect her pack. That idiotic lapse had put them all in jeopardy. He'd never forgive himself if something happened to her because he'd gotten distracted from the real reason they were back so soon.

"I'm ready," she said, when she'd finished.

He took her arm again and led her back down the corridor, this time toward the external airlocks. The slight tremor he felt running through her body had him cursing himself for an idiot again. *Nothing will happen to you*, he promised her silently as he scanned the corridors. *I will kill anyone who tries to hurt you.*

THE FRIGID AIR stole Gina's breath the instant they stepped out of the airlock. While she'd shrugged into a parka and snow boots, the sudden sharp cold of the wind bit through the heavy material. It was even colder out than the day she'd arrived.

"So a walk probably would have been a bad idea," she muttered. Alex's soft snort made her cringe.

She threw her pack over her shoulder then stuffed her mitten-covered hands into the pockets of the parka. Her breath came in a visible cloud. The wind blowing through the mountains announced the coming of a storm according to the morning's weather readings. She had to admit, the idea of leaving before the storm arrived appealed to her.

She glanced at Alex and the very thin pair of gloves he wore. "Are those going to be warm enough? They don't look like they'll protect your hands from this weather."

"They'll do," he said, his gaze scouring the landing pad from where they sheltered against the airlock's outer frame.

"But your fingers—"

"Will be fine. I can't use the blaster with thick gloves."

"Do you need to right now? We're almost at the ship."

He faced her, his gaze intense. "Your life is more important to me than a little cold. I promised I'd protect you. Stop arguing with how I do it. Trust me."

She stared into Alex's eyes for a moment, and realized he was deadly serious. Trust him? She could do that. She nodded and asked, "Now what?"

Alex returned her nod with a sharp one of his own, then looked back toward the landing pad. "Now, we go to the ship, contact our associate, and prepare for liftoff." He kept his gaze trained on their surroundings as he spoke. His alert stance had Gina examining the area too. She studied the shifting snow covering the landing pad between them and the silver and black ship, the flat expanse of snow beyond the ship before the hill sheared off into a deep valley, the rugged sweep of mountains beyond that.

Nothing. She couldn't see anything unusual. Until a huge, black shape rose up beside her.

Gina stifled a screech as Alex swung around, blaster raised. The figure stepped away from the wall, dropping the hood of his parka. Alex cursed and pointed his blaster toward the sky.

Gina blinked.

The large Binnean smiled.

At least, that's what she assumed that particular expression was when a Binnean did it. It wasn't really a comfortable expression for a human to witness. With silky black hair covering his bodies, a long, thin nose in a brown-skinned faces, and startling green eyes, the Binnean, despite his bulk, didn't look particularly dangerous—until he smiled.

The Binnean murmured something in a voice too quiet for her to hear but loud enough to make Alex chuckle. "Bin-Ral, this is Gina Xanacovich. Gina, En-BinRal Ol Binda t'Clav. He's been your guard for the last few days."

"Pleasure," she said, instinctively stretching out her hand before remembering that the Binneans had a different custom for greeting someone new. She shifted her hand to point upward, palm facing BinRal. He smiled again and gently placed a huge, brown, six-fingered fist against her palm.

"See anything?" Alex's voice cut into the greeting, turning the atmosphere serious again.

"No one. But there's evidence of a ship landing beyond the ridge where the perimeter sensors were shot out. There were tracks in the snow leading to the sensor line from the landing site. The tracks belong to a single human male. But at the perimeter, the tracks disappeared. No sign he moved back to the craft either. He could be using a glider on silent."

"Or there's at least two of them and the second one flew their ship in after the sensors were shot out. No sign of a second landing at the perimeter, so that means the ship must be small enough to hover and still pick up a passenger. AX47 D series is capable of that."

"So's the new JUP-3."

"Either way, they're both too small to hold more than three people. At least we're not outnumbered."

"Unless they had another ship waiting to be signaled in after the perimeter sensors were disabled."

"Damn," Alex breathed, letting his gaze travel over the landing pad again. "We need to leave. Now." He unzipped his parka enough to reach inside and pull out a small, flat comm-link. He pressed an area on the card, waited a beat, and Gina heard the static-laced sound of Nathan's voice acknowl-edging the call. "Get down here now, Nate. We can't tell what kind of company to expect."

Gina frowned, turning her attention to the valley just the other side of the landing pad. What was that? It wasn't a noise exactly. More like a vibration. She strained to hear against the peel of the wind. "Alex?" She tapped at him, without taking her eyes off the valley. He waved away her hand, still talking to Nathan. "Alex," she said more firmly, taking hold of his arm and squeezing through the thick mate-rial of his coat. "What is—"

Before she could finish her sentence, a small white-blue ship rose up from the valley. Except for the cloud of hot air escaping from the thrusters, the ship blended perfectly with the background. In fact, if she hadn't been watching, she might have missed it. It hung silent for an instant.

Then a bolt of white light lashed out from the laser cannons beneath the ship's hull.

53

CHAPTER EIGHT

THE SLEEK, SILVER AND BLACK SHIP ON THE LANDING PAD rocked with the force of the impact from the mysterious new ship.

"Goddamn it." Alex raised his blaster but at this distance, he couldn't come close to hitting the attacking ship. BinRal raised a huge blaster cannon from somewhere—inside his parka?—and aimed at the ship. His first shot skipped across the top of the hull, deflected by a shield. The laser cannon fired again, this time melting a black hole across the top of Alex's ship.

Still cursing, Alex shouted into the comm-link, "Secondary shields up!"

And BinRal fired another shot. This one sizzled the shield on the attacking ship, but didn't come near the hull.

"Get inside, now!" Alex shoved her back into the airlock just as another shot slammed into his ship. The secondary shields crackled as they absorbed the shock, turning an unhealthy shade of green. "Shit, they're not gonna hold. What the hell is that ship firing?"

"I don't know," BinRal answered, calmly aiming his shoulder cannon for another shot. "But I'd like one."

The last thing Gina saw before Alex and BinRal dragged her into the airlock was the orange flame that erupted when the shields on Alex's ship buckled under the onslaught. The airlock sealed, a steel door banged down, and Alex was shouting into his card again. "Terminate complex destruct sequence, Nate. We've got serious problems here."

Nathan's voice came back out of the card, clearer now that they were inside the house. "Destruct sequence terminated. Auxiliary defenses coming online." There was a slight pause then, "Fuck. They've destroyed the ship. Looks like we move to plan C."

"What happened to plan B?" Gina asked as they strode down the corridor, back toward the interior of the house.

"Plan B just got blasted all to hell by that blue ship."

"Oh," was all she could say.

Nathan stepped out of the control room to meet them. All of the equipment used to monitor the area, the house, the landing pad, and the weather was located in the single room.

"Tunnels?" Nathan asked Alex, his face a blank mask. He'd sounded as angry as she'd ever heard him over the comm-link, but now he was emotionless and all business. He was scarier this way. She flicked a glance at Alex and had to suppress a shudder at the iciness of his gaze.

"How far away is your ship?" Alex focused on BinRal, but she could see his mind ticking through their options.

"Two kilometers beyond the perimeter sensors. But it'll

be difficult with the storm approaching. The tunnels won't get us near enough."

"Biosuits?" Nathan suggested. "We've got three in the tunnels."

"Only three?" Gina felt her throat closing up.

BinRal smiled. "I'm from a hearty clan, Ms. Xanacovich. We're adapted to cold temperatures humans would consider severe."

She nodded, trying to swallow past her panic. Her ears felt strange, blocked, like she was underwater. The sound around her faded until their voices sounded like they were coming through a wall. She clenched her jaw, trying to pop her ears without much success.

"Are the biosuits necessary?" she murmured. When no one responded, she tried again, louder this time. "Alex, are the biosuits necessary?"

Three pairs of eyes focused on her. "Yes. Storm's too dangerous without them."

"No." She straightened her shoulders and sound came rushing back.

"What do you mean 'no'?"

"I can't wear one."

Alex's face stilled, his features losing all expression. "Can't? Or won't?"

"Can't. I can't. There has to be another way." Her gaze skipped over the faces of Nathan and BinRal before settling on Alex. "My father didn't tell you that part, did he?"

"You tell us."

She took a deep breath and ran a shaky hand over her eyes. "Remember the remains of the things, the M-SIDs, that were…in Jack Nevel's blood? They're micro-molecular scanning interface devises, M-SIDs for short. They were part of an experiment conducted by our team."

"Your father filled us in," Alex said impatiently, cutting her off with a sharp hand gesture. "The M-SIDs interface with biosuits. You, Jack, and the other two, Barry and Mira, had these micro-molecular scanners injected into your blood stream. A biosuit activates them. We understand. And when we started, we didn't think biosuits would be necessary. They are now, so you're gonna have to deal with it."

"You don't understand." Gina tried to keep her voice even and calm, despite her rising panic. "The experiment had unforeseen side-effects. Trust me on this. You do not want to put me in a biosuit."

"I thought these things were just like sensors, scanning your biochemical state and feeding it back to the biosuit." Alex moved closer to her and gently grasped her shoulders. She barely felt his touch through the thick material of the parka.

With a deep gulp of air, she looked him in the eyes and said, "They induce telepathy."

His breath came out in a whoosh, and he dropped his hands to his sides.

She looked down so she wouldn't have to see the expression on his face, knowing already how he felt about telepathy. "It's not a natural state, and it didn't happen to all of us. Only Mira, Jack, and myself. Barry didn't have any reaction. But because it's not natural, we can't control it. I think it's amplified too. From the research we've done, natural telepaths don't…experience the same things the three of us did." She took a stuttering breath. "If I put on a biosuit while the M-SIDs are still in my bloodstream, I'll be able to read your minds. I won't be able to block it, or ignore it, or control it. We've been trying."

The silence around her was a physical pressure, and she felt something give inside her. "You have to understand, finding sufficient funding for micro-machine and nanotech research has been harder to come by since humans exchanged inter-stellar drive systems for Binnean molecular scanning technology. Our work was mostly theory and speculation until the Farseaker Foundation gave us a grant."

A hiss of breath made her glance up. Nathan was scowling, fingering a spot on his chest, beneath his shirt. She frowned but continued her explanation. "They gave us full funding for three years. It was a dream come true, but it also gave us a very tight schedule. We tried to take every precaution. We ran a million computer simulations and droid experiments. But the time came when we had to run human trials or risk running out of money before the work was finished."

She wrapped her arms around herself, cold despite the parka. "To reduce legal risks, we decided to use volunteer members of the team first. If the trials were successful, we could move on to volunteers outside the lab. We had to bring my mother in to monitor our medical condition during the trials in order to get my father to agree to let me participate. Everything was fine. At first."

Her voice dropped off and silence filled the corridor. She had to look up to see if the two men and the Binnean were still there. Nathan and BinRal looked thoughtful, concerned. But she could tell Nathan was already running through alternatives to the biosuit option. Ever the professional.

Alex, on the other hand, looked shaken, confused, and

very angry. She'd never seen him so close to losing control—despite her best efforts to get him to lose his temper over nonsense arguments. After what he'd said to her while she was watching the riot, she knew he hated the idea of anyone being able to read his thoughts. Now she was telling him she could.

So much for chemistry.

An alarm sounded from the control room. Nathan, with BinRal on his heels, pushed between her and Alex. Alex remained in the corridor, staring at her.

"How could your father let you do that to yourself?"

"It was my choice. I knew there were risks, and I was more than willing to take them. I still am to see this work completed. But the risks shouldn't have been this severe. We were worried about the M-SIDs malfunctioning and making the suit produce too much heat or cold, or try to increase our oxygen or nitrogen levels too high. Something along those lines. We never considered that the M-SIDs might interact with our physiology. They're just supposed to scan."

"The ship's firing on the building now," Nathan called from the control room. "Small controlled bursts aimed at the doors. Fortunately, they're not trying to bring the place down on top of us." He appeared in the doorway. "But the defenses aren't going to hold out forever. We have two choices. We can run or we can fight. Without the perimeter sensors working, there's no telling how many of those ships are out there."

Alex looked at the floor, silent for so long, Nathan said, "Alex?"

"Are there any other side-effects," Alex said, looking up at her, indecision evident in the creases on his brow. "Physically, will you suffer in any way?"

"I'll have a killer headache when the biosuit comes off. Until then, I'll be physically better off than you. But I've never had the suit on outside of the lab, or for more than twenty minutes. I don't know what will happen with prolonged exposure."

He hesitated again, staring at her. "If we stay and fight, we risk losing you. Your father hired us to protect you."

"He also hired us to protect what you're carrying." Nathan's voice was quiet, directed at Alex more than her.

"We have another alternative," BinRal said. "I could go for my ship while you hold out here. We could rendezvous near a tunnel exit."

"You wouldn't have any back up," Alex said. "You won't be able to contact us once we're inside the tunnels."

"Alone, I'll move faster. I'll have a better chance of reaching the ship unnoticed."

"Sounds like the best plan D, Alex," Nathan said just as another alarm sounded from inside the room. He ducked inside, reappearing an instant later. "Defenses still holding, but we're running out of time."

Alex hesitated a moment longer before nodding. "BinRal, we'll meet you in three quarters of an hour at tunnel G. We'll hold here for as long as we can so you can contact us if you need to. They may be scanning link frequencies, so use the secure channel and code."

BinRal turned and disappeared down the corridor without a word. Alex continued to stare at her with an expression she couldn't read. She stared back, not knowing what to say.

Nathan broke the silence. "Alex, I think we need to talk."

"Later." Alex took her arm and started down the corridor.

"Keep an eye on things outside, Nate. We'll be back in a minute. Buzz me if there's an emergency."

From behind her, Gina heard Nathan mutter, "What the fuck do you think this is, Alex, a party?"

Alex ignored the comment, tugging her along until they were out of sight and hearing range. Then he turned on her.

———————

CHAPTER NINE

"WHY DIDN'T YOU TELL US ABOUT THIS SOONER?" ALEX demanded. "Something this…this big is important to know if we're going to keep you safe."

Gina shrugged and leaned against the corridor wall. She hadn't wanted to tell him after finding out how he felt about telepathy. But too late for regrets now. "I assumed dad told you I couldn't use a biosuit. The telepathy part is classified. Neither of us was supposed to discuss it. No one outside of my team and my parents know about that side-effect. My father's even kept it from the Board of Directors. We're trying to work out a way to control the reaction, temper it."

"Why? Why not just eliminate the effect, like any other bug?" He leaned a shoulder against the wall next to her, putting him close enough that she could feel his heat along the entire right side of her body.

She turned her head so she could look at him. "That was our original intension. Who would willingly use technology that opened up an unwanted, and to tell the truth, disorienting and painful new sense, which couldn't be controlled? Then one of the team pointed out how dangerous this could be in the wrong hands, this ability to hear other people's thoughts."

"And that didn't make you *more* determined to eliminate the bug?"

"It probably would have if the conversation had stopped there. It didn't. We wound out the possibilities for hours, and then someone mentioned the Shifters and the rumors that they communicated via telepathy, and wouldn't it be great if our technology allowed real communication with them."

"Communicate how? Why? They're just animals. Dangerous animals."

"Some people would argue that point with you," she murmured.

"You?"

"Me." She lifted her chin, met his gaze. The topic was so volatile it wasn't something to discuss lightly. She was trusting him more than logic said she should just by telling him which way she leaned on the issue. But since she was already trusting him with her life, a part of her knew she could trust him with this. Even if, on a personal level, it drove him away.

She shook her head, raised a hand palm open. "Whether the Shifters are dangerous or not, whether they're telepathic or not, this technology could give us the ability to finally answer some of the questions. If it can be controlled."

"Can natural telepaths read thoughts as easily as you can with the micro-scanners and a biosuit?" He was leaning closer again, his voice low.

"From what I understand, no. The few we've been able to find and interview, anonymously, said they never realized they had this trait until they met another telepath. They might hear a passing thought or murmur that didn't seem to be their own, but most wrote those off as imagination. Even with another telepath, they don't seem to be able to communicate well. None of them could do what Jack, Mira, and I did. Fortunately for them."

"Without the suit on to interface with the M-SIDs, they remain inactive?"

"Yeah."

Alex sighed and his shoulders slumped. "Why haven't you removed them yet?"

"We tried, but they disassembled on removal. Another bug. Until we work that part out, we decided they were just as well where they were."

"So without a suit on, you can't read minds?"

"No."

"Probably a good thing."

Alex's blue eyes darkened to a stormy gray, and Gina had to suck in a breath. He didn't look angry anymore. "Why's that?" she asked before she could stop herself.

"Because you'd probably run screaming if you knew what I was thinking right now."

"I doubt it. I don't scare that easily."

He grinned, and Gina shivered inside her too warm parka as much from relief as from the lure of that grin. "You're a fascinating woman, Ms. Xanacovich. I'd like the chance to get to know you better when all this is over."

He leaned close, and Gina held her breath. The touch of his lips against hers was feather light and so temptingly brief she moaned.

"God, Gina, don't do this to me now."

"Me?" Her eyes fluttered open. "What am I doing?"

"Driving me insane," he growled, his voice thick and rough.

Then he kissed her again, hard, pulling her shoulders around so that her body was pressed against his full length. His kiss fulfilled every promise her fantasies had been making since she'd first laid eyes on him. Just the feel of his lips firm against hers, his tongue sweeping hot temptation into her mouth, made her dizzy. How much better it would feel if they got rid of the damned parkas. She reached up to the zip of his jacket, but when she would have tugged, Alex broke the kiss and set her at arm's length. His breathing was ragged and harsh. He closed his eyes and took several deep, slow breaths.

When he finally opened his eyes, he said, "I just broke a rule I've lived by for years. But I've wanted to kiss you since you first stormed into your father's office spitting acid and fire. Now isn't the time. But later, when the job is finished, you and I will get back to this."

He wasn't asking. He was promising. She nodded, her heart hammering. She could hardly wait.

He dropped his hands from her shoulders and gestured back toward the control room. "We should get back to Nate."

She silently followed him, her mind reeling. She hadn't been kissed like that in a very long time, and when this was over, she intended to take him up on his promise. If they survived.

THEY'D BARELY REACHED the control room when Nathan came pounding out. "Move it," he shouted. "They're breaking through the outer locks."

Alex grabbed Gina's hand and raced down the corridor. Nathan followed, blaster raised, scanning the halls as they retreated to a part of the house that Gina hadn't been able to explore thanks to the complex system of locks and checks installed. Alex swept a lock with his comm-link, pressed his palm to a prints and DNA scanner, and looked into the needlepoint light of a retinal scanner. The locks clicked off, and the door hissed open, revealing a steep spiral of metal stairs.

"Down," he ordered her then held the door until Nathan had passed into the dim stairwell.

Lights flicked on as they moved lower. The walls of the stairwell were cut from the mountain, flickering blue-gray in the dim light. They hit the bottom of the shaft and turned toward one of the six corridors branching off from the circle of ground at the base of the stairs. Nathan pulled a small tube from the pocket of his parka and shook it. The corridor flashed to bluish visibility, the roughly cut stone of the walls wavering with shadows.

"Won't they see the light?" She nodded at the tube over Nathan's head as Alex urged her down the dark tunnel with a gentle touch to her back.

"Door sealed behind us," he said. "By the time they get through, we'll have passed too many turns."

"Unless they skip subtlety and blow the door off," Nathan muttered from ahead of them.

"True. But the door can take a lot of fire power before

giving," Alex said, putting a hand on her shoulder. "It should hold long enough. We'll just have to hurry."

She nodded, but her thoughts had skipped ahead, finally pin-pointing something that had been fidgeting at the back of her mind, "How'd they find this place?"

Alex and Nathan exchanged a look over her head. Her gaze narrowed, but before she could question them, an explosion rocked the walls of the corridor, raining a fine mist of blue-gray dust over them. "There goes the door," Nathan said without emotion.

"Keep moving." Alex squeezed her shoulder again.

She was officially worried now. But something was still nagging at her logic. "The guy you left behind, he was trustworthy?"

"He wasn't the one that gave away our position."

Stunned by the utter calm in Alex's voice, she said, "You know? You know how they found us."

"We leaked the information."

"What?" She spun on Alex as her voice echoed up the corridor.

"Quiet," Nathan hissed, before grabbing her arm to pull her along.

She jerked her arm free and held her ground, the full brunt of her glare focused on Alex. When Nathan grabbed at her a second time, Alex warned him off with a look.

"We have to move, damn it. Now. They'll have heard her shout. If they've got a triangulation scanner, they already know which tunnel we're in."

Alex ignored Nathan, but he did start her moving again with a hand at her back. "We did what we had to do to draw out the inside man on your team." He spoke quickly and quietly, ushering her along at a trot. "We ran up against some serious walls and safeguards that we couldn't bypass."

"You were only there four days! You didn't even warn me."

"We didn't expect them to beat us back here."

"So, I'm going to be tortured and killed because you didn't expect them to be quick."

"Nothing is going to happen to you." Alex pulled Gina to a halt and hauled her against him, bringing his face down to hers. "Nothing. I swear it."

Gina blinked at the fire and determination in his gaze. All of her outrage drained away.

"Let's go."

She didn't resist when Alex urged her on again. They picked up speed, and she had to jog to keep up.

CHAPTER TEN

Disoriented by the wavering tunnel shadows and the quick pace, Gina kept her head down and concentrated on moving. When they reached the end of the tunnel, she was startled by a dead-end of nothing but rock.

"Now what?" she asked, struggling to catch her breath.

Nathan stepped to one side of the tunnel and pressed a spot on the rock. A hologram disguising the tunnel exit fell away, revealing a metal door barely large enough for the men to get through. Dim light filled the cavern, revealing a plexi-sealed room with three biosuits hanging on the wall.

Gina blanched at the sight of the suits.

"We'll only use them if we have to," Alex murmured, close to her ear. "We'll hold out here for BinRal as long as we can."

"Storm's hit," Nathan said from a small computer console near the door. "We won't last long out there without the suits."

"Only if we need them. Nate, check the tunnel."

Nathan disappeared the way they'd come, and Alex moved to the console.

"What are you doing?" She moved up behind him.

"Setting the auto-destruct. We've got fifteen minutes before the rendezvous with BinRal. Whether he's here or not, we'll have to leave."

"How much time are you giving us to get away?" She wrapped her arms around herself, warding off the cold seeping through the walls.

"Twenty minutes."

"Is that enough time if BinRal isn't here in fifteen minutes?"

"It'll have to be."

"You may as well turn that off."

At the sound of the new voice, Alex spun, blaster raised, a strong arm pushing her behind him. Nathan stood with his hands up, a blaster to his head, half blocking the figure behind him. The woman in front of Nathan, however, stood in full view with a wicked looking weapon pointed at Alex's chest.

Gina choked on a curse and clenched Alex's free arm. "Mira?" She could hardly believe what she was seeing—like looking at a ghost. Mira was supposed to be dead, killed in the public link accident that had also killed Barry. All three of the other members of the team who'd had the M-SIDs injected into their blood stream were supposed to be dead.

The woman smiled. "Hi, Gina. Surprised to see me? I'm afraid only Barry made the train that day. Lucky me. Thanks for that shout, by the way. Made Louis's job pinpointing the tunnel easier."

Gina felt her lip twitch with a snarl. All her shock and

fear were buried under outrage as she watched a woman she'd trusted point a blaster at Alex. She tried stepping around him, but he held her in place with one hand, never taking his gaze off Mira.

Mira laughed, a light, relaxed sound. "Gina, that temper of yours is going to get you killed."

On a good day, Mira was an attractive woman, maybe a little small, a little too skinny, but she was an exceptional engineer. Gina had liked her and considered her a friend. "You want to try it, Mira? Put that blaster down and face me, and we'll see who gets killed."

"Face you in hand-to-hand? You really do think I'm stupid. I heard that in your thoughts, you know. How highly you rank my intellect compared to yours."

"Is that what all this is about? You think I insulted your intelligence?"

Mira's face lost all trace of emotion. "I'm paid too well to take this personally, Gina."

"By who and for what?" Gina tried to move around Alex's arm again, but he wasn't cooperating, as usual.

"Influential and rich people. Because you should have eliminated the telepathy bug in the M-SIDs."

"Another corporation?" Alex asked.

"This is bigger than corporate war. The uncontrolled spread of telepathy through the populous would cause chaos."

"Government?" Alex's question made Mira's mouth twitch.

"Influential and rich," she repeated. "In a position to make sure this telepathy doesn't get out."

"You got rid of your M-SIDs?" Gina asked. She pushed at Alex's arm again, testing. He didn't budge.

"I don't have to now." Mira tilted her head. "You should have encouraged your father to sell the technology when he had the chance."

"Why would I want to do that?" Gina's gaze danced to Nathan and the man, Louis, standing behind him. Louis was watching the scene, smiling slightly, ignoring the mercenary. Mira's attention seemed more on Gina now than on Alex. If she could just distract Mira and Louis a little more, she'd give Alex and Nathan a chance to take them down. Knowing Alex was going to hate this, she dodged in front of him before he could stop her.

Mira jerked the blaster toward her. "Stop."

"Why? You're going to kill me anyway. I'd rather die fighting than let you subject me to the torture you described in those messages."

Mira's brown eyes slanted. "What the hell are you talking about?"

"Gina," Alex hissed. Taking a step toward her.

She ignored him and focused fully on Mira's confusion, moving so Mira was between her and a potential shot from Louis, but so that she was blocking Alex from Mira's blaster.

"The messages my father's been getting. Detailing the accidents, the torture and death meted out to members of the team."

"I don't know about any messages. And stop moving or I'll blast a hole in your chest."

"If you didn't write the messages, why are you here?"

"To collect on payment due to me. I deliver you to my well-funded associates, they hold you for ransom, and your father calls off the research. Simple. And I make a lot of money."

"Your associates aren't going to ransom me, Mira. They're going to torture and kill me."

"Gina." Alex's voice was a growl now.

"You don't know what you're talking about," Mira snapped.

Gina saw that stubborn look come into Mira's eyes. Recognized it from too many late night arguments in the lab. She switched tactics. "Do you still hear it?" She dropped her voice to a murmur. "That first time, the sounds of so many voices in your head."

"Shut up. That has nothing to do with this. I'm being trained. I'll never have to suffer that way again. There's a lot of money available to the properly trained telepath."

"This is all about money for you? You can just ignore the killing?" Mira's stubbornness was one thing, but Gina couldn't understand the woman's willful ignorance. The more she refused to accept the truth, the angrier Gina got. "Didn't you hear about Jack? How your employers tortured him before they killed him?"

Mira's blaster wavered. "He probably deserved it," she spat. "He probably didn't cooperate. That's all you have to do, Gina. Cooperate and nothing will happen to you. They're just going to keep you until your scanners destruct and your father agrees to their terms. That'll be the end of it."

"You can't believe that? Not after Barry and Jack." Gina moved another step forward, keeping Mira's body between herself and Louis. "And what use will you be to them when your scanners destruct?"

"We've already altered that part of the program in my M-

SIDs. After all, I was the one who wrote the time-limited destruct algorithm."

"Damn it, Gina," Alex hissed, "get out of the way." She sensed his movement behind her but didn't dare turn away from Mira.

Louis shifted his blaster from Nathan's head, aiming at Alex over Nathan's shoulder.

"I wouldn't try anything funny, Mr. Alexander," Mira warned. "I wouldn't want to have to kill her. Drop the blaster. Now, or I'm taking her leg."

Gina heard the clatter of metal against the stone floor behind her. Mira smiled.

"Feeling better now, with both men unarmed?"

"I'll feel better when you shut up." Mira steadied the blaster. Gina watched her clicked it to a high stun setting and aimed.

Gina prepared to take the shot. It was going to hurt. She couldn't avoid it. But maybe she could give Alex and Nathan a chance at Louis and Mira. She balanced on the balls of her feet, smiled at her former colleague, and lunged.

She tried twisting aside as the blaster bolt arched toward her, but the shot caught her arm and sent her spinning. Air exploded from her lungs. The shot stole any control she had of the lunge, but her momentum slammed her into Mira. They crashed to the floor, Gina a numb heap on top of the struggling woman. She could feel the press of the blaster against her side, even through the parka, but she couldn't move to defend herself.

The last thing Gina heard before she blacked out was the sound of her name echoing off the walls.

CHAPTER ELEVEN

ALEX SETTLED INTO A CREVICE AGAINST THE SNOW COVERED mountains with Gina's limp body draped across his lap, trying to keep them out of the worst of the blowing winds. She was so still in his arms, his heart hurt. Checking the biosuit monitors, he knew she was breathing. But watching that bitch Mira shoot her had taken years off his life. And made one thing very clear.

He wanted a hell of a lot more with Gina than a few weeks of lust.

But first she needed to wake up.

He leaned against the snow bank and shifted her around so he could watch her face through the helmet's clear visor. He desperately wanted to stroke her cheek, to lay kisses across her closed lids. *Come on, Gina, come back to me. Wake up, baby.*

Glancing up and searching the snow for any sign of Nate and BinRal returning, he allowed himself a moment to wonder what would happen when she did wake up, now that

77

she was inside a suit. Would she really be able to read his mind?

The idea should bother him a lot more than it did. Just days ago he'd considered telepathy an abhorrent invasion of his privacy. Yet, as he thought of Gina being able to see into his thoughts… Of all the people in the universe, having this one woman read his mind was both dangerous and, surprisingly, okay. He had no idea what she'd find in there. That gave him pause. Would she run screaming from the man he was if she could see that deeply into him? Would his feelings for her push her too far? He knew she wanted him. She'd put herself between him and a blaster—stupid ass move though it was—and he'd never forget that bravery. But watching her get shot had tipped a fine balance between control and anger. He was dangerous like this. If she woke up, read those blood-thirsty thoughts, would he ruin any potential between them?

Maybe the M-SIDs would take a while to kick in. Maybe they'd have a few minutes before she could read his thoughts, a little time for him to…explain.

He ran a hand along the side of her helmet, the closest he could get to a caress, and watched her breathing. As her eyelids began to flutter, hope rose up to clog his throat. *That's it. Wake up.*

GINA? Come on, baby. Come back to me. That's it. Good, girl. You can do it. The litany ran steadily and comfortingly through her mind as she struggled past the blankets tangling her brain. The first thing she noticed beyond the voice was the strange taste of the air. After a moment, she felt the gentle pressure of sensor pads pressed against her pulse points. The sound of wind raged around her, but it was muted and distant.

She was in a biosuit, outside, in the middle of a blizzard.

She opened her eyes and launched herself upward.

No you don't. A firm hand eased her back down. "Gina? Listen to me, honey. It's Alex. Are you okay? Can you hear me?"

She blinked against the white-blue snow and turned to focus on him. He was wearing a biosuit too. They were out in the middle of what looked like a snowfield in a pocket at the side of a mountain. There was no sign of the tunnel, Mira, Louis, or Nathan.

"What happened? Where's Nathan?"

I can't believe you did that to me, and now all you can think about is Nate. "He's fine. He's with BinRal, and they're on their way. BinRal's ship was sabotaged. That's why he was late." *Damn, but I need to kiss you. If you ever do anything like that to me again, I'll wring your neck.* "As for what happened…"

Gina frowned, slowly realizing she was hearing a lot more than he was saying out loud. "I can hear your thoughts," she whispered, not sure whether the mike in her suit would pick up her voice. It must have because his expression shifted to a different kind of concern.

"I thought you might. I wasn't sure. I was hoping the scanners wouldn't activate so quickly."

"Only takes about thirty seconds. And I'd love to kiss you too, but lifting the visor in this weather wouldn't be wise. What happened to Mira and Louis? The house?"

His thoughts came at her in a tumble of emotions and

images that she couldn't sort through and was embarrassed to try after the first few rather graphic images formed. But his thoughts of sex were easier to take than the deep emotions churning in him.

"I disarmed Mira after you were stunned. Nate had to kill Louis. Unfortunate, since we could've gotten information from him." He shrugged. "We didn't have much time. There were more people in the house, so we had to get out and blow it fast." *I wasn't letting anyone else near you.* "We put you in the suit to protect you from the weather and the worst effects of the stunner shot. The destruct was down to five minutes by the time we were ready to go." *I almost killed that bitch for shooting you.* "We tried to get Mira into a suit to bring with us. We were hoping to pump her for more information. She gave us a bit to go on," *thanks to you,* "but I suspect the one orchestrating all of this will disappear now." *There's no place he'll be able to hide from me.* "Mira started screaming when we tried to put her in a suit. Went berserk and ran back up the tunnel. She didn't have time to get out before it blew." *And even if she had, I'd have killed her eventually.*

"Am I still in danger?" Gina frowned as she tried to sort through the chaos of his spoken and unspoken comments.

Not while I'm around. "I doubt it. The person or people that bribed Mira don't know what she's told us so they can't risk coming after you again." *I'll eat them alive if they think they can hurt you.*

"So, I'm safe as long as you're around?"

"Yeah. You are."

"Then, just exactly how long are you planning on being around?"

"You can read my thoughts? You tell me."

Gina closed her eyes, searched through the chaos of images and words, half phrases and feelings racing through Alex's mind.

When she found what she was looking for, she opened her eyes and smiled. "That long, huh?"

His answering smile warmed her more thoroughly than any biosuit ever could.

Thank you for reading
INTERFACE (The Naravan Chronicles 2).

If you've enjoyed this book, please continue reading for
an excerpt from the next story:
SECRET

CHAPTER ONE

"What the hell is that?" Dr. Ti'ann Jones squinted at the new image materializing on the molecular echo imaging readout screen. Ambient heat filtered in through the tent canvas, despite the temp regulators to keep the equipment cool, and she absently swiped at the sweat dripping down her temples. She poked a finger at the screen, indicating the scroll of elements that made up the unexpected object. "That can't be right."

Her colleague, Dr. Krin Freemont, glanced between the finalized view of the odd shape and the molecular readout table, a frown marring his nearly perfect dark caramel complexion. He pushed a shock of red hair out of his eyes and shook his head. "I have no idea what that is." He leaned back, the movement making his canvas chair groan.

"You're the genius. No miraculous leaps of insight here?"

Krin chuckled. "Hey, whatever that is, it's not a plant and

it's not geological, therefore, it's not in my realm of expertise."

Ti'ann spared him a quick glance then grunted. She considered the heat trying to defeat the cooling system and wondered if it was affecting the readout. They hadn't had any trouble so far, but that didn't mean the MEI hadn't decided to malfunction. She swung around to a secondary unit and started a diagnostic run, just to make sure everything was working properly.

"You're the paleo-zoologist." Krin gestured at the list of molecules that comprised the object. "It's got genetic material. It's organic, whatever it is, and it's sure as hell not plant life. That makes it your field, Dr. Jones."

"That," she turned back and poked the screen again, ",is not like any fossilized animal I've ever seen, heard of, read about or seen in any historical data. On or off this planet."

But she had to reluctantly agree with him. It was organic. The genetic material was native to Narava, but it was also composed of elements she'd never encountered in an animal, living or dead. Ever.

A beeping sound alerted her to the end of the diagnostic run. "Damn. The equipment is working fine," she muttered. "So, whatever it is, we're getting an accurate reading." She frowned at the image again, the mystery of it was as frustrating as it was fascinating. "You know, if it weren't for the genetic components, I'd swear that was a structure. Pyri-Stone and Quinn's Beryl Crystal is in the ground all around this area. Perfect building material."

"But even the earliest human settlers didn't build here. Especially that deep underground."

"What if…?" Ti'ann bit her bottom lip as an image of

Narava's controversial native species, the Shifters, flashed through her mind—their long golden bodies and the multi-colored swirling eyes of their natural forms. She met her partner's jade gaze. "We could always ask—"

"No." He cut her off with a sharp gesture and straightened in his seat.

"You don't even know what I'm going to say."

"I know you better than you know yourself, Ti'ann. You think this has something to do with …*them*."

"Well, what if it does?" She lowered her voice and leaned in close to him. "Someone from a Shifter support group might know what we're looking at."

"No. You do not want to bring that kind of attention to our site. There are fanatics on both sides of the extermination argument. Especially with the current Senate debates. You don't know who might land here."

"There's a friend of a friend of a friend I can contact."

"No," he repeated. "Even if you can trust this person, their presence will attract attention. We'll end up with fanatics, protesters, politicians, news reporters…" He shuddered at the mention of the last group. "All of them trampling our site. Not to mention the possible violence. No."

"Do you have any other ideas?"

"Yes. We ignore this thing." He flicked his hand toward the screen. "And we get back to the rest of the dig."

"Can you really do that? This could be the biggest thing we've ever found. It could make our careers."

"Or it could be nothing at all."

"And we won't know which until we dig."

"So we dig. Without calling in outsiders."

"What if it's dangerous? Neither one of us has even a

guess what it is. I don't want to unleash some as of yet undiscovered Naravan disease or hibernating monster because I didn't check all possible sources for information." Their jobs had always been complicated by a lack of good data about this planet's ancient history, so they had to be extraordinarily careful in their searches.

"What makes you think supporters will know any more than we do?" Krin challenged.

"The only way we'll know is by asking."

He groaned and turned to stare at the closed tent-door flap. "You're determined to contact these people?"

"I can't ignore this. *We* can't. You know we can't. Look at it. It's amazing, impossible. But I don't want to start digging if it turns out this is something potentially dangerous. We'll keep the arrival of this outside help quiet. Only you and I need to know the truth about their affiliations." She grinned and ducked her head to catch Krin's gaze. "Come on. You know you want to."

His reluctant smile made her chuckle. But when he faced her fully, his expression was serious. "Okay, we'll do things your way. But I want one concession. If you do this, we bring in security for the site."

"We don't have the funds. The grant barely covers our expenses as is."

"A friend of Devin's has some connections," Krin suggested. "It won't cost much."

"That doesn't sound entirely legal."

"You want to contact a secret support group and you're worried about legal?"

"Krin…"

"This is about keeping us all from getting killed." He

launched up out of his chair and started pacing around the tent. His circuit was short with all the equipment in the way. He paused when he heard voices from just outside the tent then continued to pace when the sound faded away.

Ti'ann had never seen her best friend this agitated. Not even when he'd been contemplating the serious step of proposing to his partner Devin, or when he'd faced possible expulsion for punching his supervisor while pursuing his third Ph.D.

"You're really serious about this?" she asked. "You really think we need security?"

"Yes." He stilled and faced her. "I think if that anomaly has anything to do with *them*, we're gonna need all the help we can get."

"And what makes you think this man will be neutral on the issue? What if he sympathizes with one side or the other?"

"He's paid to be neutral. It's what he does. That's the whole reason I'd rather hire someone like him than go to a public security firm or to the Guards."

She rolled the end of her long braid around her fingers and pursed her lips. After a silent moment, she nodded. "Okay, Krin, if you honestly think we need security, go ahead." She turned back to the readout screen and focused on the anomalous shape causing all the trouble. "But you're responsible for coming up with a way to pay him. I'm not stealing artifacts or coughing up hard won grant money."

She heard Krin's sigh of relief and almost smiled.

"I'll take care of everything." He left the tent without another word.

"Dr. Jones." One of the volunteers, Micca, stopped beside Ti'ann, drawing her attention. "There's a man here to see you."

Ti'ann stretched her back until her spine popped, sighed, then wiped the purple dust on her hands over her green khaki pants. She glanced up at the sky. The sun had arched past its zenith, starting its afternoon dip toward the horizon, but the valley was still awash in bright, hot light.

"Who is it?" she asked Micca, blinking at the young woman.

"I don't know. Dr. Freemont just told me to come and get you."

"Thanks."

When Micca turned and walked away, Ti'ann looked back at her dig site and the small animal bones she was unearthing. Their white coloring glowed in the dark purple grit covering the valley floor.

She activated the scanners surrounding the area she was working on, covering it with a magnetic blanket shield to protect it from being reburied by the sporadic winds that blew through the valley. Collecting her memo tablet from the large rock she'd set it on that morning, she nodded to the nearest person still carefully dusting specks of purple from an unclassified thigh bone and crossed to the lift platforms that carried the crew up from the valley floor to the campsite.

As the lift rose, she wondered if the members of the Shifter support group had arrived already. James Monroe, her contact in the group, had insisted on bringing several people with him, something that made her a little more nervous about her plan. She was glad Krin had insisted on security now. Keeping the reason for the presence of a small group secret was a lot more difficult than doing so for a single person. And that was just among her own team. Bringing in a group might well attract the attention of just the type of people Krin was afraid of.

But she wasn't expecting Monroe and his people for another three hours or so. It could be the security guy. She had no idea when he was expected. Though, she'd be surprised if Krin called her up for that. The security was officially Krin's responsibility. She was in charge of the Shifter support group. That suited her just fine. She was anxious to find out what their anomaly was, excited about the potential. The mystery of it had occupied her mind all morning, and she could barely wait for Monroe and his people to arrive.

As she walked down the rocky path leading from the lifts to the campsite, she pulled out her memo tablet and called up the list of elements making up the anomaly. Puzzling through the strange mixture of molecules, she only looked up and noticed her surroundings when she heard a hesitant cough. Blinking, she realized she'd reached the very edge of the camp and had nearly walked right past Krin. She started to smile.

Until she spotted the man next to Krin.

Her breath locked in her throat. She froze, unable to move or think or speak. Even when Krin stepped forward and made the introductions, several heartbeats passed before what he said worked its way into her brain.

"He's the man I was telling you about," Krin said, a note of hesitance in his voice.

She pressed her lips together to keep her mouth from dropping open and focused on Krin.

"Dr. Jones," he continued, despite the creases marring his smooth forehead, "this is Nathan Longfeather. He's agreed to assist us with our security issues."

Ti'ann nodded and was about to say they'd met before when a deep and, unfortunately, well-remembered voice said, "It's a pleasure to meet you, Dr. Jones."

Her gaze snapped around, locking with his dusky, green-amber eyes.

He didn't remember her.

She saw it in his expression, as plainly as if he'd pulled a knife out and shown it to her before plunging it into her gut. Oh god, he didn't have any idea who she was.

She suppressed the sudden tremors sneaking up her body and sucked in her top lip, pressing it hard with her teeth.

When he extended a hand at the introduction, she took it but pulled away from the warmth of his big palm with a jerk. She couldn't look him in the eyes, but letting her gaze wander over the rest of his face didn't help either.

He looked exactly how she remembered him—strong, high cheekbones; sharp, broad nose; sensuously firm lips on a wide mouth; smooth brown-red skin.

His straight black hair hung nearly to his waist, almost as long as her own. The top was held back from his face by a small braid.

His broad shoulders and narrow hips hinted at a temptingly masculine physique. Though, through his loose trousers and flight jacket, a person would have to guess at the degree of muscle and strength.

Unless that person had seen him out of his clothes.

Ti'ann's mouth dried at the memory.

She turned her attention back to Krin, so she wouldn't have to confront the man who appeared too often in her dreams. She clenched her teeth together and tried hard not to let the hurt show. But a quiet voice, deep inside, whispered, *Of course he doesn't remember you. Why would he, Ti'ann? Look at him. He's gorgeous. The kind of man most women would die to have. Why would a man like that remember someone like you?*

"I wasn't expecting him so soon," she muttered flicking a glance at Nathan before settling back more comfortably on Krin. Actually, she'd had no idea when he was expected. But she had to say something, anything to fill the void. Krin would start to worry if she didn't. And speaking to Nathan right now, when her chest felt tight and her stomach hollow, was impossible.

"I was told the situation required my immediate attention," Nathan answered. "And as I was between jobs, I had time to make myself available at the request of a friend."

There wasn't even a hint of the discomfort or embarrassment she was feeling in his voice. Just a relaxed confidence, edged for business.

Ti'ann took a deep breath and stiffened her spine, turning back to Nathan. "I'm not sure how dire our situation is, Mr. Longfeather. But Dr. Freemont thought it best we have some security. You came highly recommended from his friend."

She tried raising her voice above a mumble. But meeting his indifferent gaze was almost more than she could take, so she turned her attention to the tablet in her hand, pretending to focus on the row of anomaly data still on her screen. If she didn't have to look at him, she could pretend he was just an ordinary person, that she wasn't affected by his presence any more than he was hers. She could pretend he wasn't the man who had turned her world upside down three years ago and ruined her for all other men. She might even be able to convince herself her heart wasn't being crushed by the loss of an impossible fantasy. Lying though, even to herself, had never been one of her strengths.

Attempting a distracted tone, she said, "I assume Dr. Freemont's told you we won't be able to pay you out of our regular source of funding."

"We've already discussed a price and method of payment, Dr. Jones," Krin said, the tone of his voice hinting to stay away from the topic.

In her present state, she was happy to, as long as she could get away from Nathan Longfeather as quickly as possible. "Fine. In that case, I'll leave the particulars to you two. I'd appreciate it if you didn't interfere with the dig sites themselves, Mr. Longfeather. Otherwise, do what you think is necessary." She kept her focus on her memo tablet, running a finger over the screen to call up more data as she walked past the men toward camp.

Nathan stopped her with a statement directed to Krin. "Would you mind if I spoke with Dr. Jones alone for a few minutes, Dr. Freemont?"

Her stomach tightened in panic. She couldn't be alone with him! Not yet.

Krin must have seen panic on her face when she snapped her gaze to him because he hesitated.

"I'm sure whatever you have to discuss with Dr. Jones can be discussed with me as well, Longfeather. We're partners."

"I understand. I just have a few questions for the doctor before I begin my survey of the area."

Krin held her gaze in silent question, waiting for her to make the call.

After a moment, she nodded. "They could use a hand at the secondary site," she said to Krin. When he continued hesitating, she added, "I'll meet you in the imaging tent in half an hour."

The appointment seemed enough to settle him. He extended his hand to Nathan. "Thanks again for coming on such short notice. Find me after you've done your initial survey." To Ti'ann, he added, "I'll see you in thirty minutes."

When they were alone, Ti'ann took a deep breath and faced Nathan. She kept her gaze on a spot just beyond his right ear. But the avoidance made her feel like a ninny, so firmed her shoulders and met his gaze. "What did you need to ask me, Mr. Longfeather?"

"First, call me Nathan. *Mister* Longfeather doesn't quite work on a man in my profession."

She nodded but didn't comment.

"Second, I'd like to know what you think I should expect here."

"I know it isn't entirely normal for a paleontology dig to require security, but it's always better to be safe." She studied her tablet again, so she could drop eye contact. She was not a good liar. Or so Krin always told her. "We're awfully close to Gremblewreath and we've had a few joy riders buzz by. Since the town is known for having a less-than-law-abiding element, we don't want to risk any of the equipment getting stolen or vandalized."

"I wasn't called all this way because of Gremblewreath

thugs, Dr. Jones. I don't come cheap. There's a reason you and your partner have decided to hire my particular brand of services. But to do my job effectively, I have to know what I'm facing. What I'm really trying to secure."

She tried for a casual shrug, which felt stiff and insincere, and said, "You're here to secure this dig site. Some of our finds can be quite valuable in academic circles." Her gut tightened when she glanced over her tablet at him. He wasn't buying her story. She hated, *hated*, feeling so off-balance and uncertain in front of him. She was a professional damn it. Just because he didn't remember her, didn't mean she had to let him know he upset her.

He shook his head and settled his hands on his hips. "Keeping something from me is going to make it impossible for me to do my job, Dr. Jones. Enough of the bullshit, if you don't mind."

She narrowed her gaze and, for an instant, indignation overwhelmed her hurt and self-consciousness. "I was under the impression you were both neutral and discrete, Mr. Longfeather."

"That's what I'm being paid for."

"Then all you need to know is that you're guarding my dig site. All of it. You're here to make sure no one from the outside hurts my people."

"And just exactly who would want to hurt your people? Given this is just a paleontology dig."

She cursed silently and focused on the memo tablet again. Not only did he make her feel like an idiot, now he was making her act like one. "Mr. Longfeather—"

"Nathan."

She ignored his interruption. "The details aren't important. We scientists keep our discoveries close to the chest. Suffice it to say, we may—or may not—have found something of great interest. The find has the potential to cause some…complications. To avoid possible difficulties, Dr. Freemont felt we needed your brand of help. And if you're prepared for any kind of trouble, then that's really all the information you need right now." She held up a hand to stop him when he started to speak. "I am not prepared to go into any more details at the present. You're just going to have to deal with the information I've shared." She forced herself to look up and meet his gaze. She might feel like an ass right now, but she was a professional. And her work was too damned important to her to let him intimidate her. Or at least to let her intimidation show. "Am I clear?"

To her surprise, her outburst earned her a crooked, devastating grin. Ti'ann felt all the horrible hurt and mortification wash back over her, burying the strength she was desperately clinging to.

"Clear," he said.

His deep voice sent a skittering of desire down her spine, causing an unwanted rush of memory. The dark, cool hotel room, tangled sheets, sweat and lust, the hard strength of his body above hers, the brush of his long hair across her breasts. She blinked and took an involuntary step away from him, her throat tight from a combination of pain and longing.

"Good," she said, but even to her, her voice sounded strained. She swallowed and forced out, "Any further questions can be directed to Dr. Freemont."

"I'll do that, Dr. Jones."

She jerked out a nod and turned to leave, but his husky voice stopped her.

"By the way, do you have a first name?"

Pain lanced through her. She kept her back to him so he wouldn't see how devastated she was by his simple question. "Of course."

"Would you mind telling me?"

The last time he'd asked for her first name had been under very different circumstances. Standing here now, with him politely curious, she felt like that other time must have happened to someone else. The sexy, blond woman she'd tried to be all those years ago was someone from a dream, with no connection to her real self. Why would Nathan see that woman in the person she was now?

Straightening her shoulders, she kept her attention on the trees in front of her as she said, "Ti'ann."

Nathan said something under his breath, but she was too busy hurrying toward the safety of camp to hear him.

"I thought it was you," Nathan murmured to Ti'ann's retreating back.

He could hardly believe it was her. And of all places to meet her again, in the backwaters of Narava. He almost hadn't recognized her. She'd had blond hair when they met three years ago. And her clothes, then lack of clothing, had kept her lush body on display. With her now brown hair pulled tightly into a long, thick braid, her curves hidden in loose pants and t-shirt, and her sexy gray eyes focused on everything but him most of the time…it was hard to see the woman he'd spent those spectacular, erotic nights with. He'd had to hear her name to be sure he wasn't imagining things.

He watched the natural swing of her hips as she walked

away and his gut tightened as detailed fantasies began mixing with memory. She'd pretended not to know him just now. She was a crappy liar. He'd seen the spark of recognition before she'd attempted to mask it. She hadn't forgotten their time together any more than he had. Why she pretended they didn't have a past was a mystery he'd get to soon enough. When they had some privacy.

For three years, he hadn't been able to stop thinking about this woman and their two brief nights together. Despite his best efforts. For a few months after, he'd even considered trying to track her down.

He hadn't.

He kept telling himself it was best he'd left when he had. She was the type of woman a guy could fall hard for, and at that point in his life, he couldn't afford the distraction.

If only his ex-partner, Alex, had followed the same advice. Falling for Gina had nearly gotten them all killed. And Alex had always been the one telling Nathan not to seduce clients! Dumb bastard had gone and broken his own rule. Then married the woman! To be fair, Nathan liked Gina. She was good for his friend. And what had happened hadn't been her fault. He put the blame solidly on Alex's shoulders. But as far as Nathan was concerned, the fact that his friend was ridiculously happy with his wife did not make him any less of an asshole.

Breaking up their partnership after all the years they'd worked together hadn't helped endear Alex to him either. Even if it had been the right decision. When Nathan saw Alex these days, he took great pleasure in rubbing the ex-mercenary's face in his idiocy. Since Gina thought their banter was funny, Nathan didn't even feel guilty about the abuse he heaped on Alex.

Thoughts of his ex-partner made Nathan frown. Until that moment, he'd had every intention of seducing the lovely Dr. Jones again. Though the first time, he hadn't known she was Dr. Jones. In fact, he hadn't been able to get her name out of her until the first time he'd made her come. Knowing her name didn't make any difference, though. Then or now. Then, he'd been too busy driving them both to exhaustion.

Now?

Now, he wanted… No, he *needed* to see if the passion they'd experienced in those two nights could possibly happen again. He had never experienced anything like it, before or after. Lust so intense, so drugging, he could barely keep his hands off her. He'd had to leave the suite a couple of times just to avoid exhausting her unconscious.

He smiled thinking about it. She'd actually kept up with him quite well, if memory served.

And that was one of the problems. Was he remembering those two nights for what they were or had he blown them all out of proportion in the last three years? After watching her gray eyes flash when she attempted to put him in his place, he was pretty sure his memories were accurate. He was looking forward to confirming that, as much as he was looking forward to making her admit she remembered him.

Unfortunately, she was now his client. That was the other problem. He never got involved with someone he was working for. He actually *followed* the rule Alex had always drilled into him. When working, Nathan kept his dick in his pants.

With a resigned sigh, he accepted he was going to have to

do that now, too. For a little while anyway. He'd let Ti'ann pretend she didn't know him, and he'd resist dragging her off to his ship to prove how well she did. But as soon as this job was finished, he had plans for the good doctor.

Energetic plans.

**Don't miss the next romantic science fiction adventure in
The Naravan Chronicles Series
SECRET (The Naravan Chronicles 3)**

ABOUT THE AUTHOR

Isabo Kelly is the award-winning author of numerous science fiction, fantasy, and paranormal romances. She also writes best-selling paranormal romance under the name Kat Simons. Her life has taken her from Las Vegas to Hawaii, where she got her BA in Zoology, back to Vegas where she looked after sharks, then on to Germany and Ireland where she got her Ph.D. in Animal Behavior. Now Isabo focuses on writing. She lives in New York with her Irish husband and two beautiful boys, working as a full time writer and stay-at-home mom.

Don't miss out on new releases from Isabo! Sign up for her Newsletter here: http://eepurl.com/caxHa9

For more on Isabo and her books:
Website: http://www.isabokelly.com
Facebook: http://www.facebook.com/IsaboKelly
Twitter: https://www.twitter.com/IsaboKelly